MARY WILLIAMS

WILLIAM KIMBER · LONDON

First published in 1985 by
WILLIAM KIMBER & CO. LIMITED
100 Jermyn Street, London SW1Y 6EE

ISBN 0 7183 0577 9

Photoset in North Wales by
Derek Doyle & Associates Mold, Clwyd
and printed in Great Britain by
Biddles Limited, Guildford, Surrey

For Mike
with my love

I
1820

She had always half-guessed – half-feared – that one day Nat Herne would come riding over the hill towards Tarnefell, as he'd once ridden so frequently to Wyndecroft before her marriage to Will Drake. In quieter moments she chided herself for the idea. He had officially been proclaimed dead when his ship had foundered off the coast of the Americas. All hands, it had been stated, were lost. But she had never, secretly, been able to accept that anyone so wild and ruthless, so overflowing with vitality as Nat, was lying torn and lifeless at the bottom of the Atlantic. Merynne was happy now – happier than she'd ever been in her life. Will was kind and loving, and during the last four years had made a good father to Bethany, the daughter of her nine months' stormy period as Nat's wife, and to Luke, their three-month-old son. Will was a farmer – honest, hard-working, handsome in a burly way, with a thatch of dark fair hair curling back from a wide brow, blue eyes, and a laugh as hearty as his square-shouldered form. Not a romantic perhaps, but as real as the sun and wind and tough as Cornish earth he ploughed. Oh, she loved him. She could depend on him as a bulwark against the bitter memories of her time with Nat, and their last stormy parting.

Nat.

Whenever, at odd moments, she remembered, her heart quickened a little, and then, against her will, she shivered as though a harsh wind had suddenly seared her. Generally commonsense conquered her dark mood. She belonged to Will. Their life was rich together, fulfilled by understanding. No shadow of the past had power any more to wound her – no longings, no regrets, no doubts or fears. During the past six years a completely new existence had been founded.

Nat meant nothing to her any more.

Nothing.

But how close they had once been – how they had loved, and hated, and laughed and fought – as integral a part of the wild Cornish landscape as the gorse and heather of the windswept moors and lash of gales against the gaunt coast.

On such a day in the autumn of 1820, Merynne Drake, having helped feed the goats and chickens, made her way to the back door of the farm, Tarnefell, to prepare her husband's meal. Usually, the girl Anne, who came to assist with the children and other chores, gave a hand when necessary with the animals, but she was away on that particular afternoon, owing to her mother's illness.

The sky was dark and overcast with massed black clouds riding above the cliffs from the sea. Spatters of rain were driven on a rising wind. Above the creaking and soughing of undergrowth the screaming of a lone gull echoed shrilly as it rose with a flap of wings from a nearby derelict mine-works.

Instinctively, before entering the house, Merynne paused, and glanced eastwards. The leaden light was already fading, giving the immense scattered boulders and standing stones of the moor a menacing quality as though relics of a bygone civilization were about to come to life again, encroaching upon the present. Merynne drew the salty tang of air deep into her lungs. This country was her homeland and in her blood. She had no fear of its untamed quality, its challenge to the present. Only a few miles away, at Wyndecroft, she had been born, the daughter of a mining captain and engineer, and his wife Maria whose father had been a sea captain.

'She could've done better,' natives had said of Merynne when she'd eloped with Nat. 'A real beauty like her, and that no-good adventurer. It'll end badly, no doubt of et. A shame, an' with others so ready to take her as wife. They say that young preacher fellow at Zillar was more'n eager t'wed her. An' her only seventeen. Oh ais – a shame 'tes, an' no mistake.'

Shame or not, for the first weeks Merynne and Nat Herne had been wildly happy. Nat had gone daily to Wheal Chace, five miles west of Wyndecroft, and ten from Tarnefell, there to work long shifts in dark levels for tin, as a tut-worker. Both his parents were long since dead. Then, suddenly, one day he'd left and announced with a grin on his mouth and challenge in his eyes, that he was tired of burrowing underground like any blind mole, and was going fishing instead. But the boat he'd bought with their few savings had proved unseaworthy. After that he'd taken to peddling and visiting more kiddleywinks and fairs about the district than was necessary. His quick mind had an aptitude for making money through devious channels; his charm had a buccaneer quality that fascinated women, enabling them to part with their gold without a qualm.

Merynne at first had accepted his wanderings and the presents he brought her – shawls, trinkets, jewellery, in all innocence, until one day he was charged by the authorities for some minor offence, and brought to court. He'd been discharged on that occasion through lack of proof. But the incident nagged him, and remained in his memory.

'In America', he'd said to Merynne, more than once, 'men like me – good miners – get paid well – and are treated with respect. Think of it – gold in the pocket, and no worrying over the future for our child –' He'd broken off, with a sparkle in his dark eyes, and the certain gleam of adventure about his lips that was beginning those days to disturb her.

'But, Nat –' she'd said, 'so far away, and such a big strange place! Aren't we happy here then? You could go back to Wheal Chace, or Stonecross – I've heard they're wanting engineers there now –'

He'd shrugged and scowled. 'Not me. Not any more. I've had enough of working for greedy owners here. One day, love –' his face had brightened, 'I'll be off, and you'll have all the silks and satins you want. A fine lady that's what you'll be –'

'And what about when you're away? Or shall I go with you?'

'*You?* A woman? Don't make me laugh, girl. In time, yes. I'll send for you. Think of that. Eh? My young wife, a beauty – come to put all the foreign girls in the shade.'

She'd sighed, and her small chin had taken a stubborn thrust.

'I don't want to go to America. I want to stay here with folks I know. Oh Nat, forget it.'

But he'd not forgotten, nor had he tried, and after that the quarrels had started. He'd visited inns more and more frequently, returning to Wyndecroft in the early hours of the morning, having galloped many miles and drunk too much on the way.

Afterwards he'd always been repentant.

'I love you, Merynne,' he'd insisted, 'remember that. Nothing'll change it – *nothing*.'

She'd believed him, known it was true – in a way, but gradually, resentfully, she'd had to accept the other side of him – the devil that got into his blood, driving him to wild unpredictable actions sometimes, in search of a dream that was beyond her.

Why couldn't he be satisfied with what they had, she'd wondered as the days passed. They had so much. There was nothing he couldn't put a hand to for a living, if he was pressed. And their home – their roots were here – roots sprung from the unfettered moorland hills – the gorse, heather and wanton winds lashing the sea to fury against the lonely horizon. This was their heritage, their freedom.

Contemplating life elsewhere had seemed somehow impossible, yet she'd known if he'd wanted it she'd have gone with him.

But he hadn't wanted her.

He'd just announced one day after a fierce argument that he was sailing that week, and the next morning had gone.

Staring across the bleak moor now, she remembered with sudden clarity the emptiness left by his departure. The birth of Bethany was only two months away. She'd longed for the baby, because it would also be Nat's. For a time afterwards, she'd resented its existence. But when the child was born resentment had turned to possessive pride. The little girl was so like Nat – dark-eyed, rosy cheeked, with a passionate will and a charm that entranced all who saw her. Because of her beauty, Merynne was strict with her. *Never*, she insisted to herself frequently, should she be allowed to follow in the wild footsteps of her father. She would be trained from her earliest years to obey, and have proper values in life. Thinking of her daughter had warmed her to the attentions of Will Drake, whom she'd met frequently on Market Days, or any local fair or celebration; learning to love him had come easily to her, and as she forced herself more and more to erase any lingering longing for Nat, a certain warm gentleness had replaced the lively wild streak in her own nature.

Something of the young girl still lingered in the slender lines of her figure; when her molten cloud of fair hair was released from its pins, falling loose about her cream-white shoulders, she had the appearance of some fey, lovely elusive creature of legend, reborn to enchant and allure. Her eyes, greenish-blue, lit with specks of gold in the sunlight, slanted upwards above delicately formed nose and tilted mouth.

Yes, Merynne Drake was still beautiful, despite the rounding of hips and full bosom of early maturity. She knew it herself, although also realising that to dear Will, her looks were not of primary importance. What counted first and foremost was their deep mutual companionship – their capacity to give and take, both physically and emotionally, without doubt or questioning, romantic speech or extravagant gesture of desire. This was enough; and yet – standing there in the dying light with the rain stinging her cheeks, from the rising wind – something strangely exciting and apprehensive claimed her. It was as though the mad passions of past years momentarily obscured the present, riding in a swirl of darkness over the moors – phantom legions brought to life from the dead.

It was then she saw him. A dark figure on a black horse, taking shape from the clouds as he rode towards her, galloping heedlessly over stones and pools, past bog and lumbering granite rocks. Instinctively, she retreated into the doorway of the cottage, shaking her wet hair back from her face, one hand pressed to a breast in panic. It must be imagination, she told herself, – a vision, or dream. It couldn't – *mustn't* be Nat Herne. In a wave of panic she rushed into the hall – pulled the bolt on the door, and ran through into the parlour. Pausing in the shadows, she watched through the blurred window, the rider rein and jump from his mount. He stood for a moment, staring, then put his hands to his mouth and called:

'Merynne – Merynne, I'm back. Where are you? Merynne –'

She stood motionless as a statue, with her heart thumping painfully behind her ribs. Gripping his mount he strode savagely up the narrow path to the door, rattled the knob, and thumped heavily, calling again:

'Merynne, come out, girl. I'm back; Nat, your husband's back to claim you.'

Still she didn't move.

Presently he turned, swung himself on to his saddle, flung back his head, laughed, and shouted, 'I've found you. You're mine, girl – remember that. I'll be back –'

'Be back – be back –' a gull seemed to echo, as it rose shrilly screaming through the storm-tossed evening.

She shuddered, and pressed her hands to her eyes. When she looked up again he had gone. Only the greyness and dark clouds were left above the lonely moor.

What was the matter with her, she wondered, as she forced herself to move. Had it been a dream? – or – what? How could Nat have returned from the dead? A ghost? But ghosts didn't shout or mock, or make claims on the living. Minutes passed as reason gradually returned. Someone had been playing a trick on her, she told herself resolutely. It hadn't really been Nat at all. She hadn't seen his face properly, except for a second in a beam of light through the cloud. The image, for that brief interim, had been clear – but the form was broader and somehow more menacing than Nat's had ever been.

No.

It couldn't be he.

When Will returned to the farm half an hour later, however, she was still pale and shaken. He noticed, and asked what was the matter.

She told him, recounting as accurately as possible what the rider had shouted.

After a first frown Will, with his arm round her reassuringly, said, 'Some conjuring fellow from the fair at Zillar probably playing a trick on you, love. It couldn't be Nat Herne. Forget it. Come on now. What about supper?'

'But, Will, supposing it *was*? Supposing – it's not seven years yet. It would mean I wasn't really *your* wife, and Luke –'

He shook his head slowly.

'Nothing's going to take you from me, girl. An' don't you let any mischief-making stranger make you think it could. There's strangers about here at the moment. Talk's been going on for some time about that old mine Wheal Mart being opened again – there was a good deal of drinking tonight in The Feathers – I looked in for a pint and had a word with Crase about his stallion, and that's where I heard it. So there's bound to be men poking about the moor sometimes.'

'Oh, I see.'

Perhaps Will was right, Merynne thought hopefully.

But later it turned out that he wasn't.

2

When a week had passed, giving no sign of a revisit from the stranger Merynne had taken to be Nat, she convinced herself that Will's explanation was the true one – in the poor light and rain her imagination had run riot. He didn't doubt the figure had been real – there were no such things as ghosts – but someone 'in his cups' had been playing a cruel game with her.

'Forget it,' he said. 'If the rascally joker appears again I'll be around to teach him a lesson. I'll see I'm back at the farm punctual from now on.'

Somehow he managed to be, although at that time of the year there were fairs to visit, ferns to be cut in the bottoms and little moor, and ditches to be attended to, potatoes had to be tilled, and picked over, fields ploughed, raked, and gates and fences put in order. Naturally during the daytime he couldn't be around the house all the time, but his sharp eyes were kept more alert than usual, and during the day time of course the girl Anne was around, and the youth Ben.

Merynne herself had little spare time for brooding. Apart from domestic work there was butter-making and cooking. Sometimes another farmer from the district looked in and had a meal with them. A pedlar called at intervals, bringing tempting trinkets and fancy goods, with news to tell from other parts of the country. There was talk, he said one afternoon, that Wheal Chace might be closing completely down the following year.

'Copper running out,' the man, Tom Goyne, said,

15

shaking his head. 'That'll mean men'll be out of work an' no end o' trouble for their families, poor things. Eh well! at such times I'm glad to be a loner with no responsibilities – legally speakin'.'

He winked. He was a small, bow-legged, bright-eyed man, with a whimsical look about him, and a tilted smile suggesting he'd experienced far more adventures than he admitted. Everyone suspected he'd sired two children Wyndecroft way, a black-eyed girl and a sturdy young boy, children of a fisherman's wife, but nothing was held against him for that. The mother had been an inn-keeper's daughter used to company and fun, and her man had been away at sea longer than at home. So what else was to be expected?

'A wily little conjurer an' no mistake,' was said of the pedlar. But all liked him. In his quaint way he was spectacular in his green long-tailed coat, cocky hat with the feather in it, and the red spotted handkerchief round his neck. He had an old donkey, Gyppo, used for pulling his rickety cart along paths and lanes. A strange affection existed between them.

'When ole Gyppo goes, reckon I'll say goodbye to roamin',' he often stated. 'Then I'll tek a wumman mebbe – someone like fat Anna of the Mariner's Rest.'

A wink and a grin always accompanied the statement. No one knew quite what to believe of Tom, – where he came from originally, or what his age was. Some said he was of gipsy stock, others Irish, and that he could be anything between fifty or sixty – a little younger perhaps or even older. It didn't matter anyway; he had become as much a part of Cornwall as the standing stones and legends of the countryside, and everyone liked hearing the bits of news and stories of his journeyings.

It was about ten days after Merynne's illusion concerning Nat that he called at Will's farm, Tarnefell. Will was a mile away doing some cutting about a large field, Starnecrow.

The usual hospitality was offered, and as he sat drinking a pint of home-brewed ale, he remarked casually, 'By the way, there's some rich furriner come to Braggas who talks of buying up that mine I was speakin' of – Wheal Chace. Funny! –' he scratched his ear looking briefly puzzled, 'he reminded me o' someone – someone far back in the past, but for the life o' me I can't remember who. A big chap – horsey, kind of, wearin' tall boots an' a cape. Black curls an' one o' them high white collar things hidin' half his face. Rich though – squandered his gold in that theer kiddleywink, the Half-Moon, as though he was the Prince Regent himself. I dunno –' he broke off, sensing the sudden stiffening of Merynne's figure, the set look of her face.

Following a short pause she pulled herself together and said, with apparent nonchalance, 'The autumn fairs are on. There must be many strangers about.'

'To be sure. Guess I was imaginin' things.'

The conversation ended there, but when the pedlar had gone Merynne felt a growing unease.

One day, when she'd finished baking she found to her dismay that Bethany had disappeared. The daily girl who'd been given the afternoon off, was out, visiting a sick aunt, and the last Merynne had seen of the child was of her curled up sleeping peacefully on a cushioned bench behind the front door where late sunshine lingered, with her toy, a stuffed animal, in her arms. The baby was upstairs in his cradle. Absorbed in her task, Merynne had heard no sign of movement – no voice calling. There'd been no patter of young footsteps or indication that the little girl had clambered from the bench and gone outside. Following a fruitless search, Merynne, unheeding of the chill autumn air, and that a grey belt of cloud was rising, ran down the narrow path of the front garden without a cloak or shawl, calling, 'Beth – Beth darling – where are you – Beth –'

Her eyes searched the moor frantically. There were so many dangers waiting round every twist and turn of the

landscape to endanger the safety or even life of a young
child. Bog holes, sudden dips behind jutting granite rocks –
misleading sheep tracks that ended abruptly near a narrow
ravine cutting sharply down to a rock bound cove and the
pounding sea below.

Time after time Merynne's anxious voice penetrated the
other sounds of nature – soughs and sighing of the wind
through the undergrowth, the faint creaking of bushes and
flap of wings when a startled bird rose out into the grey air.
Above, along the rim of the moor, bal maidens and miners –
mere dots of figures in the distance – made their ways from
the day's shift of a local mine to various cottage homes.
There was the faint echo of intermittent singing, but
Merynne did not hear. Her only thought was for the child.
As she turned a curve in a path bordered by briars and
blackberry scrub, she was suddenly startled by a child's
gurling laughter. She stopped abruptly, and then she saw
them.

Nat, holding Bethany in his arms, tickling her nose with a
feather.

Merynne, without thought, rushed forward, crying, 'How
dare you! How *can* you come stealing my child while my
back was turned? – I've been so terribly frightened –'

The anger died in her as quickly as air let from a pricked
balloon to be replaced by a giant wave of relief. She put a
hand to her throat. Bethany's young face took on a
mutinous thrust, she snuggled closer against the strong male
chest, but Nat released her and handed her to her mother. A
flame lit his dark eyes briefly then his mouth hardened.

'Steal? Me? Any gipsy could've done that. Tinkers and
such like are always on the look out for a pretty youngster to
work their sly tricks. Maybe – just *maybe* I saved our – *your*
child from such a fate.'

He waited. She felt her senses and skin burning. There
were so many things to say, to explain, and enquire about,
but all she could manage was, 'I didn't expect you. Not ever.

Never to see you again. They said you were –'

'Food for the fishes.' He gave a wry laugh. 'I know. They would. But men like me don't die that easily, Merynne. I survived all right. It was a tough fight, but I won.'

'Why didn't you let me know?'

'How? Put a note in a bottle for the other side of the world and expect it to arrive in Cragga Cove? Besides –' a frown drew his dark brows together '– I didn't aim any more to keep you on a shilling or two a week with no fun or pretty clothes to your back. "When I return to Cornwall," I said to myself, every day almost, "it'll be with gold in my pocket so that wife of mine can be toast of the county." Oh yes. I had dreams for you, Merynne. I worked and slaved in mines and round gold fields until my body ached and hands and feet were raw. There were no women either – not in any serious way. And I was a fool, wasn't I?' – the grim mouth tightened into a wry smile holding no humour – 'but then I never guessed you were so aching for a man you had to give yourself to the first one who wanted to wed you.'

Her face paled a little.

'Don't talk like that. There were years between.'

'And don't try and fool me into believing you loved him. A good fellow in his country way maybe – but not your sort. It'll never last –'

Merynne waited before replying. Then she said, 'There's no point in arguing. Will will be back soon – and I have to get Bethany back –'

'Bethany?' He laughed. 'What a name. A real little saint, is she?' He poked a finger against the child's stomach. Bethany gurgled again and reached towards him. 'Bethany what, may I ask?' Nat continued ruthlessly. 'Drake? But then you were already carrying her, weren't you, when you took off. Another thing – she's not exactly the spitting image of you *or* Drake? But look at us together, Merynne. Her eyes – her hair, and wicked winning ways. A real Herne, she is. And remember – I have rights. Whatever you choose to say or do about it, you're still my wife, and the girl's mine. Oh, I don't intend to act – yet. It all depends on how you behave. If it wasn't for the child I'd have you in the bracken, here and now. And my God, you'd like it. But I've waited long enough, and can continue for a bit I reckon. One day, soon, we'll have another talk –' he broke off; his face softened. 'You made a mistake, girl. I loved you.'

She swallowed nervously, though her eyes were hard and bright. Then, after putting the child down, she said, 'I think I've a right to know –'

'What?'

'What sort of plan you have. If there'd seemed any chance you were alive I should never have married Will, but I did, and we're happy together. I don't believe the law would give you any claim –'

'Really! don't you indeed? Then you'd better think about it.' He pulled her to him abruptly and kissed her long and hard. Against her will the rich blood coursed warm and wild through Merynne's body. Her heart beat painfully. He relased her suddenly, regarded her enigmatically for a second or two then said, 'Just the same as ever, isn't it? No man will ever set you alight like I do, and no man's going to keep what's mine. Oh don't fret – I'll keep quiet – for the present. Just so long as you behave and do as you're told –'

'By *you*?' Her temper rose again.

'That's right. I've no fears of any dull yokel of a farmer.' He turned to his horse and before jumping into the saddle, added, 'You'll be hearing from me. A little pleasure now and again between us? I guess that's fair, isn't it?'

She didn't reply.

Presently he'd gone. The echo of horses' hooves faded. Spots of rain began to fall. She lifted Bethany up again and walked back towards the farm. Her body felt cold. It was as though her whole world had disintegrated. There was not even Will to confide in over such a deeply painful and personal matter. He would be hurt, whatever the outcome.

And Bethany and Luke? She realized with a stab of painful anguish that in one thing Nat Herne hadn't changed. He was ruthless, and would have what he wanted whatever the cost to others about him. Two children would make no difference – especially one that was his, and that he'd argue he had a right to.

Had he?

She looked down at the little girl, who was tugging her hand. 'Where's that nice funny man gone?' the child's voice demanded.

'Away.' Merynne told her shortly. 'And he's not a – not a nice man. He's –'

The dark eyes blazed with an unfathomable instinctive knowledge. The red lips and dark hair that already predicted her future beauty, glowed. Mischief quivered in every line of her rosy face.

'Is he my pa, mummy? Is he?'

Merynne was too shocked for an instant to answer. Then she said, 'Don't be stupid. You shouldn't say such silly things.' She started to walk away, dragging Bethany by the hand.

'But he *said* so – I heard him,' the child protested.

'Stop it.' There was a sharper tug of the tiny wrist. 'You *know* your father. And if he hears about this –'

'Don't you want me to tell him?' The young face had sobered; the eyes became solemn, watchful.

Knowing she was treading on uncertain ground, Merynne answered ambiguously. 'He'd think you were a silly girl if you did. And you don't want that, do you? So let us keep it as *our* secret – if you promise to be good and not talk nonsense.'

'I can have cream on my jam then, can I?' The bright hopeful tones told Merynne that she'd won on this occasion with her daughter. Having to use bribery with a child was objectionable to her. But at the moment there seemed no other way.

What the end of the unexpected situation would be Merynne could not even begin to visualise. The thought of Nat had become distressing to her. At the same time, her body trembled with emotions and wild feelings she could not control.

Why – oh why had Nat come back to disturb and torment her? When she reached the farm the rain had already thickened and was falling steadily, enshrouding the moor with desolation.

Will was already back, and was watching for her from the door.

'What happened?' he asked. ''Tisn't often you go out when the girl's not here, and the babe asleep on its own?' His broad face was vaguely troubled.

'I know. It was only for a few minutes. Bethany disappeared.' She forced a little smile. 'Just when I'd finished baking –'

'Beth?' He lifted the child up in his arms. 'That'll never do now, will it? You're supposed to keep an eye on your little brother.'

She didn't answer, but when Will put her down, she turned to her mother and asked gravely, 'Can I have cream on my jam?'

Merynne nodded. She felt suddenly tired.

Later, when she went down to the parlour, after putting Bethany to bed, she paused at a landing window, staring out into the grey night. The rain was easing off again, but the clouds rolled slowly over the horizon of moors and sea in a darkening belt of grey. Her lovely eyes were watchful and enigmatic, half expecting to see a lone figure astride a stallion take form and ride as a legendary figure of long ago.

But it wasn't *so* long, after all, since Nat Herne had wooed and won her. Less than a decade ago.

And now he was back.

She sighed and went slowly downstairs.

That night Will made love to her. The experience was

warm and gentle as ever, but held little comfort, and later, when she went to sleep, the tears were damp on her lashes, though Will did not know it.

3

Before winter properly set in came the proof that Wheal Chace really was to be extended and fully set to work again. Engineers arrived from the North – investigations were speedily got under way at certain points of the old workings, to ascertain the potentialities of new levels. There was much measuring, and conjecturing where fresh deeper shafts could be sunk. Ore, it was finally decided, could still be rich enough to warrant the great expense involved. Hayley Trent, one of the most famous speculators and engineers in the country, suggested that tin also could lie beneath the copper. In short, the old mine had a new life ahead, provided anyone sufficiently rich could be induced to invest.

Herne, under the name of Frank Wellan, undertook the responsibility without question. Other 'adventurers', although on a lesser scale, were induced to follow. The natives of Braggas and Thraille, two once active mining villages which at the moment were mostly unemployed, were quick to seize the opportunity of being taken on as labourers before their future jobs as 'tut' workers.

The mine stood halfway up a slope, inland towards the opposite coast, five miles roughly from Wyndecroft and ten from Tarnefell. The area was remote, a wild valley with a rough narrow lane cutting between desolate yellowing hills. As it turned abruptly left from the main road leading to Penjust, the atmosphere became more desolate, more bereft of human life, scattered at intervals by immense rocks and boulders. There was a stream running from a derelict mine on the right, reddened from soil where ore had once been rich. Vegetation was meagre, consisting chiefly of straggling thorn, twisted gorse and sloes; but mostly the ground was barren.

Sensing its potentialities however, Nat had thought, 'My God! There's wealth beneath. I know it, and I'll have it, damme.' It was the same feeling he'd had when he'd worked and slaved in the American gold fields. He'd followed his instinct then, and won. He'd do the same now in this land where he'd been born.

He was not, inherently, true Cornish. His mother had been a tumbler-girl from a fair, his father the errant wayward son of a good family, with a handle to its name, who'd taken the girl in lust, deserted her immediately, and set off to fight in the wars with France where he'd died.

The tumbler girl who was half Spanish had managed to send a little of her earnings when she had any, to a cottage woman in the Land's End district for his keep. She herself had been taken by the consumption, and from the age of eight Nat had been set to work in any job that came along – mining, or as farmer's boy, even poaching for Bob Carne who owned a smallholding on the cliffs. He had been taught cunningly to steal at fairs, and wrestle with men twice his age in any ring available. At twenty, through devious means, he'd earned sufficient to set himself up as a stallion man, which had taken him to every corner of the county. It was during the following year he'd courted and wed Merynne.

During his years away, his form had thickened, his accent changed, and he now wore a fringe of black beard and side-burns. Except for Merynne, none had recognised him, though several had been puzzled.

'A bit like that young giant of a fellow who left Wheal Tawry an' got him a great stallion,' one farmer said to another. 'Used to call sometimes. Did quite a trade. Only it can't be *he*, surely?'

The other man gave a derisive gaffaw. '*Him?* That rascally

roamin' buccaneer who plagued Merynne Payne till she took off an' married him? Doan' 'ee be s'daft, man. That one ended up in the sea all right. An' this one is *rich*. Richer'n ole Harry 'imself they do say. Let's hope 'e's true to 'is word and gives proper employment with good pay.'

So as the days passed rumour gradually quietened and died. The bold stranger was accepted as Frank Wellan and made himself popular from the very beginning by his generosity to natives and frequenters of the various kiddleywinks in the district.

Merynne, stoically refusing to dwell on Nat's involvement with Cornish mining in the peninsula, became increasingly active about the farm. Frequently there was a tart edge to her tongue when Bethany's high spirits and bursts of stubbornness got on her nerves. Will noticed, and was a little bothered.

'Merynne love,' he said one day when she'd almost slapped the child, 'what's worrying you?'

She faced him with a look of surprise on her lovely face. '*Worry?*' she echoed. 'Why? – nothing. I'm not worried. What makes you ask?'

He regarded her thoughtfully for a moment then answered, 'You're a bit tart with Bethany sometimes.'

'She can be difficult. I have to discipline her occasionally. But there's nothing wrong, Will – nothing at all.'

There was, though.

There was a great deal.

Fear gnawed at her. Fear that Nat might appear any day, as he'd threatened, and that her own weakness would betray her. In the sullen clouds, through fitful mists and movement of leafless undergrowth against the wild ever-changing horizon, she fancied, at times, the approach of his form recklessly riding over the moor; in the wild birds' crying and booming and crashing of breakers against the rocks of Cragga Cove, the echo of his voice seemed to her to be thrown back by the wind. When Christmas came and passed without incident, however, she relaxed a little, and as February brought the pale pointed buds of celandines and first pale primroses to the countryside and headlands, her confidence in Will was reinforced. How stupid she'd been to think anything could spoil their life together, she thought frequently. Nat belonged to the past. He now must realise it himself, and was purposely keeping away. She'd heard that under the name of Frank Wellan he'd bought a small but picturesque manor house near Redlake, where he now lived, with a housekeeper to look after him. More often than not, though, he was in the Penzance and Penjust vicinity for business meetings concerning the reinvestment and opening of two mines.

Things were going well for him. In business and by mining 'adventurers' he had become accepted, though not socially – as yet. This didn't disturb him at all.

'To hell with them,' he thought, following any polite but obvious snub from Cornwall's élite. 'Wait till one of the high-hatted johnnies is down on his luck and wanting to borrow a packet – that's when I'll have him – down on his ruddy knees.' The picture of some Lord Tom-Noddy kow-towing to him had titillated him enormously. Gold was his safeguard against any ultimate humiliation or defeat. It could buy him anything he liked. Except one thing perhaps – the right to have his own wife soft and compliant in his arms. One day he would – his words to her had been no idle threat. But it had to be at the right time. In an odd way he didn't wish to hurt her. He knew he should have contacted her earlier. He should have recognised that a passionate young creature such as herself would find someone else sooner or later. But hell's fire! – she could have waited a bit longer surely.

It was in such a mood that on an early spring day he rode again towards Tarnefell. The air was heady and sweet; even when the sun had lifted a cloak of fine mist still filmed the bushes and heather, shrouding the line where cliffs met sea, diamonding bracken and undergrowth with cobwebbed filaments. Nat jerked his horse to a swift canter. He had no definite plan – only the urge, the compulsion to have Merynne in his arms again, taste the wild sweetness of her lips under his.

When he saw her by the ravine staring out to sea, he reined abruptly, feeling his heart quicken, and desire deepen. Her hair was blown back, freed of its pins, on a gentle breeze. From a sideways angle the curves of her breasts and thighs were visible under the blue cotton dress. She had sprigs of blossom in her hand, and something in a basket swinging from the other arm. He kicked his mount ahead again. She glanced round, startled, as he approached. In a confusion of anger and torment she felt unable to move or walk away. This was the moment she had dreaded, the inevitable meeting again with the man who'd been – or was still – her husband.

Leading his horse by the bridle, he strode towards her, tethered the animal loosely to a tree and said, facing her, 'At last! I told you, didn't I!' He put out an arm. She drew back instinctively, pulling her thin shawl tightly across her breasts. The blossom fell to the ground.

'Don't touch me,' she said. 'Please go, Nat. It's no good. Go away –'

He threw back his head and laughed.

'No good? No good? Oh, Merynne, spare me the dramatics, love, I always said you should have joined the players –'

'Don't be ridiculous. And don't mock. You're insufferable.'

'So I am. So I am,' he said, with the smile fading. 'And I'm also your truly and legally wedded spouse, Mrs Herne. Remembering might make things a deal easier for you.'

She turned quickly to take the narrow track back to the farm, but the next second he'd swung her round and her body was close against him. She struggled wildly, and with her head flung back, tried fruitlessly to break away.

It was no use.

Suddenly she was on the ground, where the tips of early bluebells pierced the damp earth. Resistance died in her as his strong hands unbuttoned her gown, then circled her breasts and slim waist above soft rounded thighs.

Close by a blackbird sang, trilling joyously from a gorse bush. Conscience and strain died. For that short interim they were lost to everything but mutual need and passion. When the giving and taking was over, Merynne lay for minutes staring at the sky. Above hers, his eyes shone. The firm lips had a stubborn look, triumphant. Merynne forced herself to get up. Her face was white.

'You shouldn't have done that –'

'*Me?*'

'Neither of us. It was wrong. I'm Will's wife.'

'Don't lie,' he said, with his expression darkening. 'It's not true and you know it. We belong. We always have. Oh come, love. Don't fight. Behave –'

'*Behave?*' Her voice rose. 'After – after – what's just happened? Lying there – like vagabonds in the heather? I'm not that sort of woman, Nat Herne, and when I tell Will –'

'But you won't, will you? Because he's kind and gentle, and a fool. If he wasn't he'd have moulded you into some sort of shape by now. As it is –' He smiled wrily.

'Yes?' Her voice was faint.

'You'll have to wait and see, won't you?' Bitterness filled his voice. 'Don't worry, wife. Everything will be arranged – in time.'

Contempt filled her voice, but not her heart, when she replied shaking her head slowly, 'Not in the way you think. You've had your own way too long. I shan't give Will up now, Nat, whatever you threaten or do. Oh, I loved you once. So much I could have died for you. But those years you stayed away killed it. You could have come back earlier – got word to me somehow that you were still alive. It was cruel of you to let me suffer –'

'Ah! but if you understood what happened –'

'I don't, and I never could,' she interrupted fiercely. 'No doubt you had a very colourful and adventurous time –'

'I was half murdered in Kimberley by a couple of cut-throats – savaged by Africans, and had all I'd worked for stolen in a whore-house,' he told her bluntly. 'More than once I had to start over again without a dime in my pocket, working myself to the bone with all the guts I had, thinking – "This is for Merynne. One day she'll benefit, as my true wife –" ' he paused before adding, 'But you *weren't* true, were you? You had to take up with the first lusting male around.'

Her lips tightened.

'Stop it. I won't listen. Go away –' She turned and half tripped, but was on her feet again before he could reach her. She walked on more carefully, aware that he was not following. When she reached the gate of a small stone-walled field, she glanced back once. He was sitting, motionless, astride his horse, like some silhouetted figure on the landscape, carved in granite.

'I shall be back,' he called. But the wind carried the words away and she didn't hear.

Will was not yet back home when she reached the farm, and by the time he arrived she'd decided not to tell him of the encounter. Many times during the weeks that followed, it was on the tip of her tongue to confess the truth. But whenever she made the attempt, she was depressed by his questioning smile, the clear very straight look of his blue eyes, and turned the subject aside by some casual excuse.

How could she hurt him, when he'd been so good to her? *How could* she bear to see his trust and buoyancy turn to doubt, bewilderment, and dull disappointment at her weakness? Somehow he would have dealt with the unsavoury fact of Nat Herne's return. But that she could so quickly succumb again, give herself so easily to the buccaneer of a man who'd neglected her for years, would have spoiled their whole life together. Despite Will's patience, he could be abnormally stubborn once an idea got into his head; he might forgive her, but she doubted he'd ever want her again as his wife. The latter thought distressed her more than she'd believed possible. All the goodness in her – the true side of her nature – loved him. But the wild part was still there – the instinctive knowledge to be possessed and subject to Herne, her first dominant love – the man who'd made the world sing when the winds and sea raged against the cliffs – who set her pulses hammering each time the warm fire of his flesh contacted hers, whose very glance was stimulus and excitement to her being.

Oh, she was bewildered and tormented during those early days of spring. Her manner outwardly was deceptive, and at moments she felt brief shame that Will could be so easily gulled. He was busy though, particularly at that time of the year, as all farmers were, and she made it her business to help him in any possible way, hiding her true feelings under the façade of hard work.

Not that she loved Nat any more, she affirmed to herself more often than was necessary. She didn't. She disliked and sometimes hated him for intruding into the peaceful tempo of her life, and kept firmly away from any likely chance meeting place. Periodically though, her eyes wandered unthinkingly to the far moorland ridge beyond which narrow tracks led westwards to the gaunt valley cutting towards Wheal Chace, fearing yet still half hoping to see Nat riding towards her on his stallion.

For many weeks there was no sign of him.

Then, when young summer came, with lush ditches and hedgerows of the valleys sweet and frothing with blossom, violets, primroses, and curling young ferns, Merynne, on her ways back from Penjust Fair, where she'd taken produce in the trap for marketing, saw the familiar figure riding from the opposite direction. At first she pretended not to notice him, and increased the young mare's speed, looking neither to right or left. Her hair was loosely blown on the wind, her thin cape thrown back over her shoulders.

'Oh God!' she thought inwardly, almost praying, 'not now. *Please* not now.'

But it was no use. Having recognised her instinctively, Nat cut down the slope sharply, and almost before she was aware of it had intercepted the vehicle by reining immediately in front of her.

She pulled up abruptly.

'What do you want?'

'You,' he answered smiling, dismounting and leading his horse by the bridle towards her.

Her hand tightened on Nelly – her mare's – reins. 'Please get out of my way, Nat Herne. It's all over.'

'What?'

'You. Us. What there was between us. *And* you know it. Why make things worse? Why try and hurt me? Haven't you done enough already? D'you want to make my life a misery by spying and waiting for me everytime I go a mile from the house? If that's what you call love –'

'It isn't. No pretence any more, Merynne. It's the real thing I'm after and mean to have – the right to hold my own woman, my wife, in my arms. I've already seen my solicitor –'

Her face paled.

'You – what?'

'My solicitor. A good man at his job – Truro way. According to him the case'll be an easy one – if you and Drake *want* a case, that is. Actually there's no need, providing you behave sensibly. By the way, have you told Drake yet? Does he know about what happened the last time we met?'

She said nothing.

'I thought not. Well, you'd better be quick and tell him, hadn't you? Or would you rather I called on him myself?'

She jumped up, dropping the reins, shocked and resentful.

'*No – no*. Not that. *Please*, Nat –' The pony startled by her quick gesture, reared, and with a sharp neigh, started off along the track, dragging the trap behind him. Merynne lurched, and reached for the reins wildly.

To no avail. She toppled and was thrown from the vehicle before it was at full speed. Nat ran and caught her as her form rolled towards a stone wall behind a ditch massed with verdant undergrowth.

Except for a few scratches she appeared unharmed. He lifted her up in his arms, peering anxiously into her face, then gently smoothed the silky mass of tumbled hair from her forehead.

'Are you hurt?' he asked.

She struggled slightly. 'No. Put me down. The trap – the pony –'

He laughed derisively. 'They're gone all right. Good thing too. You're where you belong now. In my care.' He eased her down. She gave a short gasp of pain.

'What's the matter?'

'My foot. My ankle –'

He carried her to a spot of soft short turf by the wayside, pushed up her skirt and unlaced the boot. Then his hands were about her white thighs, under the thick petticoat, easing the stocking down. A hand wildly clawed at his. Her eyes were blazing.

'Don't dare do that.'

He stared, astonished, at a scratch where a line of blood faintly trickled.

'You little demon,' he exclaimed. 'Haven't changed at all, have you? Still the same fiery little virago I once knew, for all your prim ways. If it wasn't for that cursed foot I'd put you over my knee here and now, and give you the walloping you deserve. So just behave, will you?'

'You're a brute, Nat Herne.'

'I can be, when it's necessary. Now shut up and let me get on with the job.'

He took off his neckscarf, expertly felt and examined the bruised leg, then bound it up with the linen.

'You'll have to rest it for a day or two,' he said, 'and I must get you home as soon as possible.'

'But – how? The trap's gone, and Will –'

'Oh, damn Will. Why the devil did he allow you to go out driving the thing alone – at this time of the year especially when there are tramps and pedlars and cut-throats around. You know very well what risky louts and vagabonds lurk about on fair days. Seems to me the sooner he knows where he stands the better. You too. So don't argue. Up with you.'

In a dream of wild, conflicting emotions, Merynne allowed herself to be lifted to the stallion's back, and a moment later they were galloping in the direction of Tarnefell. As the sweet heady air swept her hair in a pale stream behind her, warmth and excitement replaced fear, bringing a glow to her cheeks and heart; the breeze sang as they passed. Boulders, furze bushes, and standing stones appeared briefly and the next moment were gone. The contact with Nat's body and steam of animal flesh drove all thought from her mind, except that she was with Nat again – her first wild reckless love, and father of Bethany. The thud of the great stallion's hooves, was joy and release to her. Just for that brief interim, time died – until they reached a certain hillock commanding a wide vista of moor. She knew it well.

Nat drew his mount to a halt. Two hundred yards or so away, Tarnefell stood squarefaced and grey, halfway down to the valley. The dot of a figure – the young labourer who helped – was moving about the yard. The daily maid was probably busy in the kitchen or dealing with Bethany. Domestic routine, like a damp cloth, suddenly swept illusion away. Merynne's elation died into dull acceptance.

'Put me down, Nat,' she said. 'If I go quietly I can walk.'

'And fall again? Break a leg maybe? And how are you going to explain to your thick-headed farmer? What about the trap – the pony?'

'Well, that's easy, isn't it, something frightened it. Nat –' her manner was urgent, impelling. 'Don't press me into anything – not yet. *Please* –' Her voice was trembling. Her eyes, when she looked at him were damp and glowing with a soft violet tinge to them.

He sighed.

'All right. This once. But next time we meet it'll be for good, Merynne. You know that as well as me. So you'd better get your mind clear and think out how best to tackle Drake. I could gladly smash his face in for taking what's mine. But maybe he'd no choice, with you around.'

He helped her down, and studied her ironically. 'I could even be sorry for the poor fellow.'

'But –'

'No buts. You heard what I said. Now – try the foot.'

She did so gingerly.

'It's not too bad. I can walk. When Will knows there's been an accident he won't question anything.'

'If that's what you want. You've got him by the ear all right, poor fool. Very well. Away with you then – for the present.'

He paused before mounting, then suddenly moved quickly and swept her into his arms. The strength and urgency of his lips on hers seemed to drain all the life and sweetness from her body. 'Oh Nat – Nat –' her heart cried. 'I need you, *need* you –' Abruptly she tore herself from his embrace.

Without another sound Nat swung himself on to the stallion's back, turned and kicked it to a sharp canter, which turned into a gallop as he made for the ridge westwards.

Merynne, with a desolate sense of emptiness, took the path down the slope to Tarnefell.

She didn't know that Will, from a barn two fields to the

right of the farm, had witnessed the whole scene, and was struggling hard for self control when she entered the house.

*

He didn't confront her concerning the incident until later, over supper. She'd noted his silence, a certain moodiness, before he came to the table, but had put it down to tiredness.

He was about to tackle his beef when he put his knife and fork down, and giving her a long penetrating glance, said, 'I saw you a while ago, out there – on the moor.'

Her heart seemed to stop for a moment before racing on again at a wild speed. She didn't have to ask what he meant, it was all too obvious. He *knew*. She'd thought he was miles away doing business concerning a tithe of hay. In any case Nat's action had been unexpected, and it had been hardly likely Will would be scanning the moor at such an hour.

In a daze she heard him continue, 'The horse is back, but the trap's broken. I saw it from Braggas way. Jim Carne stopped them. I've bin looking for you, half demented I was –'

She shook her head slowly. A sense of utter desperation filled her.

'Will, I – I can explain. It isn't –'

''Tisn't quite what it appeared? Eh? No it was *him*. I c'n believe that. The filthy –'

She put her hands momentarily to her ears; her throat was dry, her voice hoarse with emotion when she exclaimed, 'I *told* you he was back. I *warned* you, but you said it was someone else – some mountebank from the fair. Why didn't you listen, Will?'

He pushed his plate away, got to his feet, and said dully, wiping a strand of hair from his forehead, 'I should have, of course. But I didn't expect you to go meeting him on the moor. You could've driven on, couldn't you? There was no need to get out and land up in his arms?'

'No. There was no need. He *stopped* me. It *happened*. And the pony took fright. I'm sorry the trap's broken. I couldn't help it –'

'Nor help the cuddling and kissing, I suppose.'

'I wasn't cuddling or kissing. I did my best to get back to you – to *you*, Will –'

Something of her distress registered; he realised she was speaking the truth, in part, anyway.

'All right, I believe you.' He walked to the window, and stood there, staring out, arms behind his back.

'Will,' she begged more quietly, 'please have your food.'

'I don't want anything.'

'But you must eat –'

He turned round swiftly and swept the plate from the table. Its contents spilled on the floor making a mess over the granite slabs.

'I say no. Do you expect me to stomach a thing, knowing that coarse philanderer's been spewing kisses all over you?'

Tight-lipped, she bent to pick up the broken plate up. 'It wasn't like that. It all happened before I knew it. No harm's done.'

'No *harm?*' His blue eyes were blazing when she got up. 'I take your word for it because I can do nothing else. Nothing, but see it never happens again. And that I will; make no mistake about it.'

'What do you mean?'

'It's no business of yours. You'll see in all good time.'

He drew a hand across his eyes, stood for a moment indecisively, watching her then went through an inner door leading to the hall which passed the dairy and curved upstairs to the children's bedroom.

The boy was sleeping in his cot, but Bethany was still awake. A small oil lamp was hanging nearby. In its glow her curls and dark eyes were touched to flame, her cheeks rosy. She smiled when she saw him, and his cold anger changed to grudging, yet fierce, affection. Since his marriage to

Merynne he'd accepted her as his, and grown to love her with all the genuine emotion hidden beneath his practical exterior. Now this roaming buccaneer, her blood father, meant to steal not only his wife but her daughter, who was the sister of his own son, Luke.

He pushed a finger to the cot, and let the little child hold it for a second or two. Then, after a quick kiss on her cheek, said gruffly, 'Go to sleep now. There's a good girl.'

'Stay and talk to me. Tell me a story.'

'Not now. I can't. Tomorrow though.'

He turned and walked away, closing the door quietly behind him.

A second later his heavy footsteps could be heard receding to the gun-room.

4

On a certain late July day, steamy with heat, windless, foreboding with the threat of thunder, Drake, apparently aimlessly, but with a gnawing purpose gradually building up in him, wandered from the farm, gun in hand, about the vicinity of the moor where he'd seen Merynne and Nat so passionately interlocked in each other's arms. He didn't doubt the meeting had been unplanned on her part, but her capitulation had been clear, and he meant to frighten that bounder calling himself Frank Wellan off for good. The man couldn't *prove* his identity – if he could – the law anyway would be on Drake's side.

At most times he was a mild man, but once his blood was up he had to face and settle issues in his own way, or there'd be no peace or reason left in him any more. Since he'd seen the couple on that fateful day things had been wrong between Merynne and him. She'd appeared dutiful and tried to please him, had submitted her body willingly when he wanted it. But underneath, the fire was lacking – the warmth that used to be there was gone. She was either afraid, or play-acting for some devious reason of her own, and he had to have things straight and clear. He was that sort of man.

He'd heard Wellan was in the locality, probing and fussing about local mines. It would be natural if he veered towards Tarnefell. So there was every likelihood they'd meet. And when they did, Will would be ready for him.

Merynne had watched him go out, and he'd been uneasy. If she'd obeyed her instinct she'd have followed him. But she daren't risk a scene. Her husband – and she still accepted him as that – had been strange with her lately; always watching. Not necessarily impolite, but imcommunicative and sullen if she questioned where he was going, or what his business for the day was.

So she continued with her practical duties at the farm, and when his figure disappeared round a hummock or moor in the distance, deliberately avoided looking that way again.

Will, meanwhile, made a pretence of examining any fencing or wiring of land belonging to Tarnefell, kept a shrewd eye open for signs of poaching, strolled seawards towards the kiddleywink, then cut upwards again and rounded the bend.

It was then, coming in a direction almost straight towards him that he saw Nat, alias Frank Wellan, riding down the track from a derelict mine. He wore black riding kit except for a flash of white neckscarf that caught a momentary gleam of sunlight from the sullen sky. Then the clouds descended again; sombre – yellowish – emphasising, to Will, the brooding quality of horse and rider.

He was looking for Merynne, of course, Drake decided with fury deepening in him. He stood quite still, waiting, with his hand ready on the gun. He had no intention of killing the man – just frightening the life out of him so he never came within a mile of Tarnefell again.

The buccaneer was a thief and a trespasser about to invade farmlands. A poacher and mountebank thinking to foul Merynne's body as he'd done in the past with his filthy hands. The very idea brought a rush of blood to his head. Everything became blurred – a lurid red before his eyes. Then, as the sound of galloping hooves registered, the landscape clarified and became vividly clear. Will moved from the stone sharply, standing darkly aggressive in the middle of the path. Startled, the horse reared, but a moment later Nat had the animal under control.

'What the devil are you trying to do?' he shouted. 'Kill

me?' He'd pulled the horse to a standstill.

There was a pause before Will shouted thickly, 'Get down. Get off that animal and hear what I've to say.'

'You fool!' Nat cried. 'Away with you.' He kicked the stallion, giving a free rein. At exactly the same moment Drake fired his gun. There was a shrill whinnying from the horse, as it reared again, flinging Nat to the ground. The animal galloped away for a distance, leaving the two men facing each other. Nat, too, was armed. He drew his revolver.

'Is it a duel you're wanting, you fool?'

Will flung the gun down. 'Fists'll do me. And when you've got what's coming to you, keep away from my wife or I'll have you limp as any shot rabbit on the ground.'

There was a moment's pause; an interim of silence more menacing than any battle of words. Black eyes held the hard, unswerving blue ones. Nat was half a foot taller than Will, but he recognised the farmer's strength and the fury of determination that possessed him. Suddenly Herne made a leap forward. His fist shot straight into the other man's face.

Will staggered, fell back, half-blinded and bleeding, but sufficiently near to his gun to seize it, and stumbling to his feet, fired it several times in Herne's direction. Then wiping the blood from his face, and vomiting, he turned only half aware of direction, or that he was taking a track towards the sinister yawning gap of a deserted mine shaft. Brambles and undergrowth covered the hole. Fencing had once been put round, but storms and the weather had almost shattered it. Local folk avoided the area, knowing of the danger to animals and unwary human beings. Even Herne himself knew of the place.

'Come back, you fool,' Nat shouted. 'You're near that damned shaft. And there's bog –'

Drake turned. A shot scared a number of birds that rose screaming into the air. Herne made a last effort to save the man. But as he plunged through the undergrowth, a number of further shots rang out. He paused, scanning the landscape. Just for a second he saw the farmer's body crumple and topple forward. Then all was silent, completely motionless; as motionless as a dead world, until heavy spots of rain began to fall followed by the first rumble of thunder.

The shaft had not claimed Will, but his own gun had shattered his heart.

Nat, known as Frank Wellan, reported later what he'd seen to the authorities, and the corpse was recovered. The official verdict reported was that William Drake, farmer, following a brain haemorrhage had gone berserk and shot himself, although whether intentionally or not could not be determined.

5

Reconstruction of Wheal Chace continued. Men from all parts of the area found work of some sort. Wellan had old cottages restored, derelict hamlets gradually came to life again. Rows of new mining cottages were built, and sanitary conditions improved on old sites. In spite of this he remained a figure of mystery and surmise. A number of older natives were still puzzled by his likeness – features and certain gestures emphasised at particular angles – to the 'ne'er-do-well' Nat Herne who had travelled the countryside years ago as stallion man and pedlar of sorts. It couldn't *be* him, of course, they agreed, whenever the subject arose. All the same there was something funny – kind of secretive about him that suggested he had something to hide. And why was he so often seen in the area of Tarnefell? Naturally, as benefactor to the district he'd want to show a helping hand to that poor Merynne Drake who'd lost her husband so tragically. But Wellan had been on the scene at the time of Will's death. Did he know more than he'd said? And another thing – voices generally lowered at this point – wasn't it peculiar, to say the least, that looking like Herne as he did sometimes, the man should show such a fancy for his widow? The one who'd gone and married Drake after the drowning?

The whole business somehow had a strange tang to it. But, of course, there was no proving anything, and in the end comments died once more into shrugs of doubt and eventual dismissal. What good could come of conjectures

anyway? And what point was there in trying to harm the
status of a man who – wherever he came from or might be –
had proved to be a blessing to so many poverty-stricken
miners?

Merynne, unaware of the few hushed comments, and who
would have been uncaring of them anyway, kept herself as
aloof as possible from the scattered country community. She
devoted herself fanatically into continuing to run the small
farm, going to market days as before, proving herself
surprisingly adept at bargaining and in business matters.
Her aloof and proud air discouraged those who'd have
offered sympathy and friendship. Women considered her
hard, and when she took on a man to help the youth – a
stranger from Padstow way – tongues became suddenly
bitter.

'Seems to've got over the loss remarkable quick,' was a
usual comment, followed by, 'Oh ais, she's got her head
screwed on proper. Maybe there was no love between them
two arter all.'

'Well, when you come to think of et –' and so on and so
on.

Nat had called twice at the farm following Will's death.
But each time he'd been rebuffed.

'I don't want to talk about it,' she said on the first
occasion, her chin lifted defiantly, her eyes icy and
condemning. 'Will's dead. Please go away. I don't need help
from anyone. He left more than you think. The children and
I won't want for anything.'

'I'll see they won't,' Nat had said sharply. 'One's mine,
remember, and none of my kin are going to be without their
due. Merynne –' his voice had suddenly softened. 'What
about it? You're free now. Your precious conscience can be
at rest. Will's gone, so –'

'Yes. Thanks to *you*.' The shrill note in her voice shocked
him.

'What do you mean?'

'You did it, didn't you?'

He'd stared in astonishment, then remarked, 'What a mind you've got, Mrs Herne. And get that into your head will you? – I said *Mrs Herne.*'

'I heard you.'

He'd grabbed her wrist so hard she'd winced.

'You'd better remember it then,' he'd said, 'because the day's coming when I'll have you warm and willing in my arms as I once did. We'll be married all over again, Merynne. Mrs Wellan you'll be then. So stop any talk about me killing your lusty farmer. I'm not that sort – or soft in the head either, as he was. Think I'd've done such a damn silly thing? Even for you?'

She'd backed into the doorway. 'Go away. Do you mind? I don't want to talk about it. Especially to you.'

He'd turned on his heel, as he'd done before and said again, 'I'll be back. If only to claim my daughter. And then see how far your high-and-mighty airs get you.'

She'd found herself trembling when he left. His very presence had roused her to such doubt, despair, longing and suspicion, mingled with guilt and grief over Will's death, that nothing seemed to register clearly any more. She couldn't rid herself of the dark thought that Nat had been responsible. Whatever the experts said, Herne was sufficiently clever and ruthless somehow to have engineered the shooting. His hand *might* have pressed the trigger. But no one would convict or even accuse him of it, simply because he had power now, and wealth. Well – she for one would prove to him that she was not deceived.

As for Bethany – her heart contracted with acute pain. He'd threatened to get her, and once he'd made up his mind over any set course she knew nothing would deter him. On the other hand, if he took the case to court, no judge would permit the young child to be taken from her mother. The farm, though small, was still paying its way, Bethany had every care and comfort, and in stating his case Nat would be forced to reveal his true identity. Much of the respect he now enjoyed would be sacrificed, and he wouldn't like that. Nat Herne was not the man to indulge in any losing game. So all she had to do was to stand firm and ignore his pleas or threats.

It wasn't easy.

Every time his horse appeared near the rim of the moor, her inside lurched, and panic seized her. Part of her still yearned and wanted him as she knew she could never want any other man. There were moments when she longed to fling down anything she might be doing, rush to him, and let his arms sweep her hard against his strong chest. But when he approached, her form stiffened, and her lovely eyes hardened.

Because of him, Will – kind-hearted loyal Will – had died. In her life, she told herself harshly, she'd betrayed him through giving herself to Nat. In death it would be different. Nat Herne should never touch her again.

In such moments of decision it was possible to keep her word. Nat called one day, and after an angry exchange of words, seized her by the arms and forced her down on to a settee in the back parlour. She lay with tightened lips, staring up at him with such icy dislike he winced inwardly.

'You must be mad,' he said. 'Why the devil are you behaving this way? Everything's set right for us now. 'Tisn't as if we're not already wed. You remember that, don't you – *don't* you?' His grip tightened on her shoulders.

'*Will* was my husband,' she said with deadly precision. 'He cared and looked after me. You were just a – just a –'

'Yes?'

'Oh let me go. *Leave* me.' She lifted an arm, thumping his chest, at the same time turning her head away.

He forced her face round and kissed her. His lips seemed to burn into her very soul. Softly, unexpectedly, she started to cry. He released her, and his voice was more gentle when he said, 'Merynne – Merynne – I love you. For God's sake don't fight. Marry me – marry me and be my true wife again. It's a nice house I've got, and Bethany and the boy'll have every chance in life. You can't go on forever alone here. Don't you see, love?'

She shook her head silently. He sighed, wiped a hand across his brow, straightened his cravat and walked to the door. He turned there and gave her a long hard glance.

'It's not over,' he said. 'Think about it and try and get things into proportion. For Bethany's sake as well as yours.'

She said nothing, just sat silently with one hand to her cheek, the other fiddling with the narrow black velvet bow at her neck. She was wearing a blueish-green dress that accentuated her fair skin and shining molten gold hair. Resenting her poise and apparent coldness, Nat went out and slammed the door. The daily girl was in the front garden with the little girl when he went out. He stopped and had a word with them.

'Hullo, Bethany,' he said, 'what've you got there?'

She looked up smiling, her eyes bright and eager. 'Berries,' she said. 'Look!'

She held out a spray of thorn with scarlet fruit clustering the lean branches which now had only a number of yellowing leaves on them.

'Very pretty,' he said, patting the dark curls. 'But don't eat any.'

'Why? They're not poison.'

'How d'you know?'

'Because Mama said so.'

'*Did* she? Well it wasn't a very clever thing to tell you. You might make a mistake and eat something else that would give you a pain another time.'

'Like toadstools?'

He frowned. 'I hope you don't go picking those things.'

She shook her head. 'Only with Mama, or Anne –' she glanced towards the girl. 'They know the *real* mushrooms.' She paused before adding precociously, 'I'm not silly, you know.'

'I'm damn sure you're not,' he thought with a pang of pride mingled with irritation.

The girl smiled. 'She's really bin taught to be careful, surr. There's not much about wild flowers and such like that young Bethany doesn' know. Seems to be a natural gift with her. Thisbe and Rom've helped too.'

'Thisbe and Rom?'

'Tinkers, surr, or gipsies, I dunno. They live by the hill, Braggas way. Sell brooms an' posies an' such like. They work hard – they've two young ones, and an old mother. The mistress takes honey from them; when Thisbe was ill last year – the master – Mr Will, surr, saw they had eggs an' a few goodies free.'

'I see.'

Little more was said following the ambiguous two words. A minute later Nat had untethered his mount and was riding away. He had no personal grudge against gipsies, but the fact that Bethany had been allowed to mix with them so freely might prove he had a valuable card in his hand to play, should matters resolve themselves into a legal battle between himself and Merynne.

Bethany, meanwhile, had formed her own opinion concerning Nat.

'He's my pa really,' she confided to Anne. 'When I'm bigger I'm going to go away from here and live with him.'

Anne stared at her in astonishment. 'Whatever story are you tellin'?' she asked sharply. 'I never heard of such a thing. A real lie. An' you know it. If you was my mother's child she'd put you over her knee an' give you a proper spankin'.'

Bethany shook her head. 'Tisn't a lie,' she said stubbornly. 'I heard Mama say something to him, an' besides, I *know*.'

'Know? How?'

The little girl thumped her chest. 'Here, inside. He likes me, and I love him.'

'Loving anyone doesn' make him your father.'

'*I've* made him my papa,' Bethany insisted. 'An' I *prayed* too.'

'At night d'you mean? Before you went to sleep?'

The child nodded. 'Mama was there.'

'An' she *heard* you?'

'Oh no. *That* part was secret. I wasn't saying anything loud about it to the good Lord, like they do in chapel, at Braggas. I just *wished* it hard, and when Mama had gone I got up again and said it to Torgale.'

Anne gasped. '*That* old thing? The stone? You prayed to that?'

Bethany nodded.

'When I want something very much I always do. Torgale knows magic. And there was a moon.'

The girl was silent. The menhir, which was of extremely ancient origin, had a carved wicked face entwined by strange curved words that no one understood. It stood entangled with thorn and undergrowth halfway up the moorland hill behind the farm, and was regarded with suspicion by natives. The legend was that in past times Torgale had been some devil-god who had witnessed dark scenes of sacrifice and cruelty. A broken flat slab of granite lay at the foot, and occasionally a dead rabbit, fowl, or some other animal had been found there, either stabbed, shot or strangled. No one had ever admitted being concerned, but many were convinced the poor creatures were sacrificed as appeasement to the ancient deity. Once the macabre menhir had been found dislodged and uprooted, lying fifty yards down the slope. It had been left there until signs of ill-luck had struck the area. Several cows had sickened and died, Eliza Casey had borne a half-wit son, and a bal maid had been killed in a surface working at the mine. After that the effigy had been taken back to its original position, and firmly embedded there, where it had remained ever since.

For some moments following the little girl's disclosures,

Anne was silent, too shocked for words, then she said in low hushed tones, 'Never *never* do such a thing again, or somethin' *awful* will happen. Something evil. The devil'll get 'ee then for sure.'

Bethany very solemn and wide-eyed looked up questioningly into the girl's face. 'I don't think so. I think you're trying to frighten me.'

'And that's as it should be.'

'It isn't then. Torgale won't hurt me. We're friends. And if ever he wasn't my friend, the nice man – my real papa – would come and give him a push so he'd go rolling, rolling, into the sea.' She laughed.

Anne shook Bethany's arm sharply. 'You're a bad girl. I'll tell your ma about you –'

'*She* wouldn't care,' Bethany said scornfully. 'She's not frightened of anything, and anyway –' she paused before adding, 'she doesn't *really* mind about me.'

'Now that's a wrong thing to say too, she loves you.'

Bethany shrugged. 'I think love's silly – from some people. Do you love anyone, Anne?'

'Of course.'

'Who?'

'My folk of course, an' –'

Bethany waited. 'Yes?'

'Oh never you mind. Tisn't your business. A real Miss Inquisitive you're becoming, an' that's for sure.'

Bethany broke free, ran away, and suddenly spied something in the grass. She bent down and pulled it up. 'Look – I've found a real one this time – a mushroom.'

Anne examined it. 'It's not. It's a toadstool. An' you know what –'

'What Mama said? And him? – the nice man – yes I remember.' She threw it down and stamped on it. The girl shook her head slowly. 'You're getting too much for me, Bethany. I don't know as it's right for me to be in charge of you anymore.'

'Oh well, if you leave I'll go too, and find my papa,' the child told her in cool, practical tones. 'Don't worry. Everything will be all right.'

But everything was *not* all right.

Through defiance of Nat and a fanatical determination to have nothing to do with him – to somehow erase his memory altogether – Merynne undertook more of the practical work about the farm, which meant that she had less time than before with Bethany and Luke. Luke, who was a placid baby in appearance and temperament very like Will, was content to be tended by Anne, and slept much of the day. Bethany's eager mind and body were forever on the alert, puzzling about something or slipping away whenever she had the chance to some nearby secret haunt on the moors where she pretended to be a legendary figure of her own imagination – a fairy-tale princess or an enchantress who could work spells.

Her games were played mostly round and about Torgale. Sometimes he was a wicked being about to capture her, at others a handsome prince, who'd been turned to stone by an evil witch. Even in late October one or two rare foxgloves still thrust fading bells through the bracken on tall straight stems. She would pull one up when she felt like it, use it as a wand, and skip round the old menhir chanting a song of her own concoction. But as the colder days chilled the life from drooping flowers and undergrowth a little of the magic faded.

'You silly old thing,' she shouted to Torgale one morning when the moors lay dull brown and grey under a clouded sky. 'You can't move, can you? You can't do anything. Not like me. You're only an old stone!' She paused, and stood quite still, staring, hoping for an instant the menhir's gnarled face would change, and that the piece of granite would come stumping towards her. But of course it didn't. She knew deep down it never would. The only magic Torgale possessed was hers – at least half of it. And no one could go on pretending and pretending for ever. So she turned and made her way down the path to the farm. Anne saw her from the door.

'Where've you bin?' she said sharply.

Bethany shrugged. 'You know. Not far – just there, up the hill.'

'By that old stone again? What you like about it *I* don't know –'

'I don't any more. I'm tired of it,' the little girl answered.

'That's good then. Come in, an' your tea'll be ready presently.'

'In a minute,' Bethany said.

At that moment Luke began to cry. Exasperated, the girl retreated with a last admonishment of 'see it's only a minute, or there'll be trouble.'

Bethany waited until Anne's figure had disappeared down the hall; then, in a fit of rebellion and desire for escape and adventure, she started running down the slope, taking a track that eventually led to the cliffs where it cut through a narrow ravine to the sea. The cove had been strictly forbidden to her; it was particularly dangerous when winds drove great waves swirling about the rocks, especially at high tide. The currents were strong there, and gales could arise without warning, sweeping stones, weeds, and any defenceless small creature to the open Atlantic. Yet on calm days the place could hold a dreamy enchantment. Tiny fish and sea animals lurked in secret shining pools – shadowed reflections from glistening green to gleaming pink and blues shone jewel-like in fitful sunlight. Bethany had been there only once when Tallan – Rom the gipsy's son – had taken her with him, gathering driftwood. They hadn't been long, and no one had found out. But she'd not forgotten the strange magical sensation of 'place', and now, impelled by her inborn longing for freedom, she raced heedlessly on, tearing her dress and entangling her hair with gorse and thorn bushes intruding over the thread of path.

Suddenly she came to the ravine. She stopped momentarily, her gaze riveted by the white froth of swirling foam below. Two small squealing figures were darting about by the edge of the sea, clambering over and around the rocks, plucking limpets and pushing them into sacks.

Tallan and Sheba – the son and daughter of Rom and Thisbe.

Bethany called, but they didn't hear. So she started clambering down the side of the ravine, following a goat track which was still visible but considerably outgrown. She was awed, but not afraid, and when she reached the cove waited for a minute or two before running ahead to join the other two children.

It was then that the unpredictable happened. During the last half hour the wind had been freshening. Suddenly an immense freak wave swept in, flooding the narrow inlets of Cragga then receding with a thunderous roar. Bethany, in a safer position than the other two children, clung to the stump of a firmly embedded tree jutting from the cliff face, screaming and terrified. But Tallan and Sheba were defenceless against the tide. For a few seconds the boy swam, and made an attempt to save his sister. It was no use. Before he could reach her another wave rolled in, claiming both. Just for a second or two their hands waved frantically from the water; Tallan's head appeared once or twice before finally disappearing. Of Sheba there was no sign at all. The sacks of limpets were tossed into the air to be left as so much flotsam at the mouth of the cave. Bethany's screaming continued, as shrill and high as the gulls crying above.

Someone sensed, or heard the frail human call.

A man.

Looking down, Nat, who had been on a visit once more to see Merynne, could just glimpse, with horror, the small figure of his own daughter clinging and half protected by the twisted branches and trunks of the old tree. He dismounted, and not waiting to tether his horse, swung himself down the side of the ravine, and was in time to catch her before her young strength gave out against the ever-increasing fury of the elements. By then even her sobbing had stopped, stemmed by exhaustion.

He pressed her gently against him, swept the wet curls from her face and carried her up the cliff. His horse was nowhere to be seen. But it took him only a short time to reach the farm.

Merynne, having missed Bethany, was searching frantically near the house. When she saw him and recognised her daughter she hurried towards them with panic on her face.

'So now you see what you've done,' he said harshly, staring at her as though he hated her.

She gasped.

'It wasn't my fault. I –'

'Get out of my way,' he told her coldly. 'My child needs comfort and something warm to drink. Perhaps now you'll see sense, leave this damned benighted farm and join me in your rightful place. If you don't – no matter. Do what you like. But my own child will live with me where she can be safe – properly cared for. Take your choice. It's up to you.'

Anger replaced her fear. 'Yes, it *is* my choice. You have no right at all to blame me or order me about. After deserting me to have a baby on my own and bring her up in the best way I knew with a good man to care for her – no law in the land would be on your side.'

'No?' A brief lop-sided smile touched his mouth sarcastically. 'We'll see about that. Think things over tonight. In the morning I'll be back for you and that boy of yours.'

'*Luke?*'

He shrugged. 'Naturally; I don't aim to part him from you; he'll have good treatment – equal with the girl – at Morningsgate. And I'll do my best to forget Drake ever sired him. I suppose it *was* Drake by the way? You didn't by any chance play fast and loose with another lusting adventurer?'

'How dare you!'

He gave a derisive cough. 'Dramatics again? Oh switch off the act, Merynne, and get on with things.' He was still holding Bethany against his chest. 'Take her; get her warm and dry for heaven's sake. And see she's properly wrapped up. The wind's changed, we shall have it against us on the way back.'

'The way back?' Her voice was incredulous.

'I'm taking no more risks. Bethany's going with me. I'll be back in the morning for you.'

'For me?'

'That's right, so see you and the boy are ready. Another thing –' his face clouded, 'those two poor little vagabonds were taken by the tide. And as far as I know I'm the only one who saw. I'll have another look in the cave, although it's a waste of time. Not a chance in hell.' He turned, strode swiftly to the door, looked back and said, before leaving, 'No tricks now. You do what I say or there'll be the devil to pay.'

There was a sharp slam of the door, and he'd gone.

Merynne stood for a moment speechless, then looked down at the small dripping figure in her arms. Colour was returning to the child's face. When she blinked and stared at her mother, her eyes, though innocent, held the challenging quality of Nat's. She'd survive, Merynne knew with relief, but she'd always be a responsibility – always wild and unpredictable.

'You're a naughty girl,' she said. 'What am I going to do with you? What now? – Oh heavens, I wish I knew.'

The self-question was futile. She already had the answer. In a short time Nat would be back for the child. And that night Merynne herself had to make a decision concerning her own life.

So it was that on the following morning, after brief temporary arrangements concerning the farm and animals had been made – Merynne and Luke, accompanied by Nat, started off by stage coach from Penjust for Morningsgate.

*

Meanwhile, at their small encampment under the brow of the moorland hills, Rom and Thisbe, who'd heard of their children's drowning from an old shepherd, Pete Bran, held a solemn grieving incantation for the dead.

The old grandmother uttered an ancient curse in a language that was strange even to her own kith and kin. She cursed the gorgios and the fates that had driven her ancestors from their own land to be forever wanderers. For a day and a night, as the fury of the elements swept North Cornwall, her cracked old voice joined the thunder of the waves and moaning of the wind.

When at last the storm cleared she slept, in complete exhaustion.

Thisbe and Rom, dry-eyed by then, went on with their broom-making automatically.

''Twas no one's fault,' Rom said, dully. 'Life comes and then goes. What Fate decides, even Romanies has to take. Soon we'll move on again. Tomorrow has much in store. No one knows what tomorrow'll bring.'

One of the bodies – Tallan's – was washed up the following day. Sheba's was never found.

A week later they were trekking northwards, unknowingly towards Morningsgate.

6

Night had already set in when Merynne and Luke, accompanied by Nat, arrived at Morningsgate. The journey to Redlake by stage coach had been stuffy and tiring, despite the chilly weather, but at The Juggler's Rest, where Nat's private chaise waited, refreshments of soup, bread and cheese, and warm milk for the wailing little boy, had revived them to a certain extent. A log fire burned in the large grate of the old inn's private parlour. Merynne was grateful to sit on a bench with the baby on her lap so the glowing wood could ease her strained nerves, and soothe the child to doze again.

Nat spent a time away from her in the tap room where he drank two tankards of beer. In spite of his bluff determined exterior, uncertainty concerning Merynne gnawed at him. Things would come right in the end, he told himself constantly – what she'd had from that yokel of a country farmer was nothing to what he'd give her when she proved herself to be a warm wife again. Maybe he shouldn't have taken her so suddenly that day in the heather, but she'd responded quite willingly, and after their marriage which would make her Mrs Frank Wellan in the eyes of society and the law – for he'd already had his name legally changed – she could start again with her head held proudly and become a respected graceful figure in the locality.

He wouldn't be mean with her, she could change and furnish Morningsgate in any way she chose. He'd allow her a free spending spree on her own clothes and personal vanities, and he'd prove as good a father to Luke as to Bethany. The restlessness in him – the inherent wild desire for adventure and change could be curbed for good, provided this one woman he desired so passionately opened her heart and body to him again as she had in the early days of their first marriage. If new challenges came their way, they'd face them together. Merynne was no stick-in-the mud – no ordinary domesticated young matron content to grow placid and bovine with the years. Oh, they'd savour life to the full, once she came to him freely, abandoning her fiery spirit to his. In the meantime, he'd be patient, and not pester her. He had a marriage certificate ready for the following week. Until then he'd respect her privacy and show she could trust him.

'Well,' he said, returning to the parlour, with a further tankard of beer in his hand, 'feeling better now?'

She glanced up. A log suddenly spitted and flared, lighting her cheeks to a warm golden glow.

'I'm quite all right,' she answered, with no expression on her face whatsoever.

'Oh.' Nonplussed, he touched her hand. She drew it away, glancing down at the baby.

'Luke's tired,' she remarked.

'He looks fit enough. On the small side of course, but maybe with more food and care he'll fatten up like Bethany.'

It was the wrong thing to have said, and the next moment he knew it.

'He's had all the care he needs; at the farm we had the best food possible, and he'll *never* be like Bethany,' Merynne said coldly. 'Luke is a good baby. Bethany never was.'

He forced a grin.

'I can imagine it. Like me – eh?'

She looked away. 'In some ways. Not all.'

'Which is for the best, I guess.'

'Perhaps.'

All traces of a smile left his face.

'The horses will be getting restive,' he said. 'If you've had what you want, we'd better be moving again.'

Merynne laid the baby briefly on a settle, allowed Nat to place her cloak around her shoulders, while she picked up her reticule. One of his hands lingered a second on a shoulder, sensing the cool skin beneath the grey fabric of her gown. If she noticed she made no sign of it, but simply discouraged any gesture of affection by fiddling with the clasp of the cloak. He drew himself up to a stiff posture, then moved away, allowing her to cross to the oak-framed mirror in order to tie the strings of her bonnet.

Luke became restive, emitting a faint wail. She lifted him up, wrapped the warm shawl round him, and holding him against her breast said, 'I'm ready.'

'Good.'

Settlement was made with the burly landlord's wife, and a few moments later they were in the Wellan chaise, on their way to Morningsgate.

'There's one thing I must remind you of, Merynne,' Nat said quietly against her ear.

'Yes?' she half turned her head.

'You must be careful to call me Frank now. Mr Wellan to the servants and outside world. That will be your name very shortly. Mrs Frank Wellan.'

His assumption provoked her to remark shortly, 'I didn't say –'

'You don't need to,' he remarked before she could finish. 'You'd hardly enter my household in any other capacity.'

The pedantic polite statement would have made her smile if she hadn't been so annoyed. How unlike the old Nat, she thought ironically – the Nat who'd so scoffed at convention and the social pleasantries. But then he'd always been capable of playing any part that suited his own aims and ambition. Adventurer, actor, business man all in one, this was Nat Herne. As Frank Wellan she knew she'd have to accept him in future, while putting up privately with the arrogant demands of the real man she knew so well.

The short journey to Morningsgate from Redlake took only half an hour. The house, which had an Elizabethan wing at one side, was mostly Georgian architecture, with a short drive leading through iron gates to the porticoed front door. From there it curved round the side of the building to the back and the stables. A pale moon lit the sky intermittently, showing hills silhouetted on the north and eastern sides, and a gradual shape of parkland to the west, dotted by thickets of dark trees. A small lodge was huddled by the side of the gates the vehicle had just pulled through – and Merynne thought for an instant she glimpsed a face staring in the wan flare of a candle. Then it was gone. Everything became clouded, and a sense of complete unreality dulled Merynne's tired mind.

It was with a returning feeling of dread that she saw the swinging motion of an oil-lamp behind the front window of her new home. The doors opened before Nat – or Frank – had mounted the six steps leading up to them. A dark-haired woman stood there, wearing a white lace cap, and white frilled apron over a black silk dress. The housekeeper of course, Merynne thought wearily. It was only when they entered the hall and in a brighter light that she realised how very handsome the woman was. The glint of tiny gold rings fluttered from lobes of ears, above which a mass of very black hair was pulled high to the back of her head. Perfectly modelled red lips gleamed against a white skin, her figure, though full, was well shaped, with a small waist.

Merynne had expected some show of opposition – perhaps even dislike. But there was none. Instead a smile curved the lovely mouth in welcome. Merynne's hand was taken in a warm grasp.

'How cold you are, madam,' the woman said. 'You must go to your room first. I have had a large fire made, and the little one –' She peered down at Luke's tiny face. 'Ah, how small he is! – there is a cradle already prepared. Then when you are ready you must come down to the front parlour for a hot meal –' She broke off, turning to Nat. 'I'm so sorry, sir, to ramble on in this way. It is for you – of course –'

'Nonsense.' His expression was warm. 'It's natural and right for you to take charge, and I'm sure my wife to be – Mrs Drake, will appreciate your services as much as I do.'

'Ah!' Again the slightly foreign gesture of a hand and note in the husky voice which Merynne had noticed instantly. 'Your wife to be. Yes. I almost forgot. The mama of little Bethany –'

'How is Bethany?' Merynne heard herself interrupting coldly. 'In bed, I suppose?'

'Naturally, madam. When you're ready I'll take you to my room and you shall see for yourself.'

'*Your* room?'

'Bethany slept with Madame Duvonne last night –' Nat said quickly, 'and well, I believe?'

'As good as gold,' the housekeeper assured him. 'In fact I enjoyed having her with me. We're already friends.'

'You see?' Nat remarked with a pleased glance at Merynne. 'There was no need to worry about the child, and if Mrs Duvonne's agreeable to continue with the arrangement it might be a good idea. Come along now, let's go to our rooms.'

Silently but with her chin set mutinously Merynne, with little Luke in her arms, followed Nat and the woman up the wide staircase to the first landing. The confusion of the flickering glow of an oil-lamp and thin stream of moonlight filtering through a gothic style stained glass window gave no clear picture of the furnishings, though an air of shabby gentility pervaded the atmosphere. As Nat had purchased the building 'lock, stock and barrel', as he put it, ancient portraits and relics of former times adorned the walls.

At the head of the stairs, in a shallow alcove, a longcase clock ticked resonantly. They turned abruptly to the left, walking on carpeting that had once been luxurious and thickly piled and was now very worn in parts. Madame Duvonne opened the third door on the left, and waited for the two to pass through. The smell of flowers filled the warm air. The furnishing was delicately feminine, reminiscent of a French period, probably Louis Quinze. Panelled walls were lit to rosy pink from the flames of a large log fire burning in a marble and gold ornately carved grate. The cradle for Luke standing in a sheltered shallow alcove near a canopied four-poster bed, was trimmed with lace and ribboned bows. Old fashioned, elegant, and somehow theatrical, unreal, Merynne thought.

'Is this really for – is this to be permanent?' she queried bluntly.

He nodded. 'If you're comfortable. Until we're married anyway,' he told her, with no expression in his voice whatever. 'All arrangements are changeable, as you should well know.'

'Yes.'

The door closed quietly behind Mrs Duvonne's retreating figure. Merynne shrugged. 'It's very elegant.'

'I suppose so. After what you've been used to.'

'Don't talk like that. I was happy at the farm.'

'So you've said before – and far too often. Well, maybe with luck and a little willpower you'll be able to adjust to things here. I sincerely hope so, otherwise it'll be damned awkward for all of us.'

To change the conversation she said coldly, 'I don't agree with you about Bethany sleeping with that – that foreign woman.'

'That foreign woman?' He laughed. 'She's only half-French, a reliable, good manager, and a very warm-hearted woman. Bethany fell for her instantly. You should be grateful; you've surely enough to do looking after your son.'

When she didn't reply, he added, 'Anyway, try and relax now. I'll see you downstairs presently, when I've got my own things sorted out. My own hidey-hole, by the way, is the end door on the right. Give a shout if you want anything – or better still, pull the bell for one of the servants.'

He turned on his heel sharply and left. She was not sure whether she was pleased or disappointed that he made no attempt to embrace or kiss her.

7

Three days passed, during which Merynne, still emotionally confused, did her best to adjust herself to life at Morningsgate. She was puzzled by Nat's attitude of aloof consideration. Since her arrival he had made no attempt to invade her privacy, and although they ate together in the large, rather draughty, dining room, it sometimes seemed to her they were strangers. At odd moments when he thought she was unaware, she caught his eyes upon her briefly holding the old fire. A second later it had gone, and he would be referring to some practical matter needing attention. She felt chilled and rejected, having no inkling of the effort caused him by stifling all the natural instincts of his reckless nature. Even when the forthcoming marriage ceremony was mentioned, it was as though they were discussing a business undertaking rather than a personal matter.

Each evening after retiring to bed she was on edge half hoping, half fearing to hear his voice at the door and the knob turning. But it didn't happen. In depressed moments of irritation she began to wonder if he was playing a game with her, trying to pay her out for marrying Will. Poor Will. Why should he though? The grudges were on her side, and naturally so. Because of him Will Drake had died; she couldn't free herself of the niggling thought that Nat – or Frank as she was learning to call him – was at the root of the tragedy, and guilt swept over her that she could even contemplate remarriage. If it hadn't been for Bethany! – but then Bethany, from the time she could walk had been a thorn in her flesh, defiant, self-willed and always a challenge. Oh she loved her, but the love was obviously one-sided. Since Merynne's arrival at Morningsgate, the little girl had shown an obvious preference for Madame Duvonne, rather than for her own mother.

'You shouldn't call Mrs Duvonne "Vonny",' Merynne said sharply one morning after finding the child at the linen cupboard with the housekeeper.

'Why?'

The question was so innocent, so direct, Merynne was taken aback.

'Because it's not – it's not done.'

'Why isn't it done? Anne was Anne, and Vonny said she liked Vonny better than Mrs anything.'

'She may. That's not the point. You don't know her very well. Children don't address grown-ups by nicknames.'

An impish smile crossed Bethany's face. '*I* do. I'm different. Anyway – Papa wouldn't mind.'

'Have you asked him?'

'No. But I shall. He'll say what I want him to. You see! And he likes Vonny.'

'Oh yes. I can believe that.'

'She knows lots of stories about adventures and gipsies and people who act –'

'The theatre, you mean.'

Bethany nodded. 'If you talked to her, Mama, you'd know what I mean. She kind of makes you sing inside.'

'Sing inside? How ridiculous.'

But even when she spoke the words, Merynne knew very well how her daughter felt. The idea occurred to her of putting the matter of 'Vonny' herself to the housekeeper. But she didn't. The woman might consider she was jealous, which would be understandable.

So she stifled her resentment, and Frank decided complacently that everything at Morningsgate was working out well, to plan. On more than one occasion he stopped outside Merynne's door when she'd gone upstairs for the night, pictured her moving quietly to and fro from the mirror to bed, her hair loose, soft and silky about her shoulders, her slender form subtly visible in the lamplight. Once he heard the tinkle of something falling – a bottle of perfume possibly, or one of the silver-topped accessories of her dressing table. Desire for her almost broke his resolve not to claim 'his rights' before their marriage, which was so short a time away, but he forced himself to walk firmly away. Let her puzzle and wonder a bit, he decided. He'd had her once since his return, and she'd proved the old flame between them was still there all right. Besides, servants talked. There could be no gossip, if no cause was given; when Mrs Merynne Drake wed Frank Wellan it would be as a young widow with no touch of scandal to mar her name.

Laurette Duvonne, of course, being half-French was a little sceptical and highly amused at his show of virtue. She was not conventional, and if he'd wished to take her for a brief time as mistress during the two months of her instalment as housekeeper at Morningsgate, she would willingly have obliged. But his heart had obviously been elsewhere, and when she'd first set her eyes on the alluring Merynne Drake, she'd quite understood. Merynne, in a shy, almost fey way, was a *femme fatale*.

Laurette knew men and women well. Before taking on the housekeeping project, she'd been 'dresser' and occasional understudy to a touring theatrical company, in which she'd learned the potential qualities of any aspiring young actress, and the feminine essentials necessary for a successful entry into the stage world. Of all requirements one quality superseded the rest – the ability to titillate male interest. Great beauties could lack it, whereas a less spectacular woman could possess it to excess. Merynne was of the latter genre. The odd thing was she didn't realise it, silly girl, unlike her young daughter Bethany, who appeared destined for a colourful future. And such a 'knowing' little thing, with such vitality and zest for learning about life. If Gaylord Werne, Laurette's late producer, could have had her, he'd be training her and making her already a child draw in one of his shows. But Gaylord, actor-manager, who'd run his company with comparative success for many years, had had to disband it some months ago.

Lack of funds and the fact that audiences were becoming weary of the old turns had forced him reluctantly to the sad fact that the fashions and taste for theatre were changing. He had not sufficient in his pocket to employ new stars on top of other inevitable expenses. When debts were cleared there would be only sufficient in his pocket to see him through a decidedly sticky time. So he'd paid off his cast and travelled about as best he could, through Britain and the Continent, doing spare 'acts' himself when the opportunity arose, as conjurer or impresario – a talented and able Jack-of-all-trades in the acting profession; the rest of the company, like herself, had found employment elsewhere and by many different means.

Always, when Laurette looked back, it was with nostalgia and faint regret; but with true French sophistry and fatalism she accepted the present, which *could* have been far worse. And there was now Bethany.

Bethany was magnetised by Laurette's stories and reminiscences of her life with the company; she had also learned to read early – a fact that had forced Merynne to decide that a governess must be found for her in the new year.

Meanwhile she absorbed avidly extracts from Shakespeare's *A Midsummer Night's Dream*, revelling in the fairy-tale beauty of Titania and mischievous Puck, even pretending to be each character in turn, including the comical Bottom.

'I would like to act on a real stage,' she confided to Laurette one evening shortly before going to bed. 'Perhaps –

if I didn't grow too big and tall like you, I could be Titania. Do you think so, Vonny?'

'I think you'll be anything you want to be one day,' the housekeeper said fondly.

'Did you ever?' the child continued. 'I mean – did you ever wear fancy clothes and act like the people you were with?'

Laurette laughed.

'Oh sometimes – just occasionally I was a vagabond or some fat old nurse,' Laurette said, with a laugh. 'I was always much too large for the important lady parts.'

Bethany considered her critically.

'You have a lovely face though. Nicer than my mother's even.'

'You mustn't say that, *ma chérie*,' Laurette remarked disapprovingly. 'Not even think it. Your mother has something – a quality about her that is very rare.'

'What quality? What do you mean?'

'Of enchantment – of allure. But that's a word you wouldn't understand yet. One day perhaps you will.'

'One day could be a very long time,' the little girl answered grudgingly. 'I want to know things now. Everything – everything I *can*. And I want to dance, and sing, and laugh, and have lots and lots of adventures. I want to be like you, Vonny –'

Just at that moment, when Laurette was about to silence her, there was a sharp tap on the door, and Merynne entered the bedroom.

Instantly she became defensive. 'So *there* you are. I thought so. I've been looking everywhere for you. You should be in bed. *Really*! –' turning to the other woman, 'I do wish you wouldn't invite my daughter so frequently to your room. She's only young, and needs her full sleep every night.'

'I'm sorry, madam. I was about to tell her to leave.'

'She didn't invite me anyway,' Bethany retorted quickly. 'I just came, because I like it here; there are books and pictures, and Vonny knows so many things. Tell Mama about Toby –

you know – the funny man in the play – Toby Finch.'

'Not now,' Laurette's voice became firm. 'Some other time perhaps, if you mother wishes me too.'

Grudgingly the little girl was led away.

'I wish you'd behave, and stay in one place sometimes, like other children,' Merynne said. 'It would make things so much easier.'

'But I'm not like other children,' Bethany retorted. 'I'm *me*. And do you know what I'm going to be when I grow up? I'm going to act and go on the stage, and be all sorts of people. Vonny says –'

'Forget what Mrs Duvonne says. When the time comes you'll do what you're told –'

'By you? Or by my Papa?' A faint tinge of slyness was in the child's voice.

'By both.'

'But you don't get on, do you?'

Merynne gasped.

'That's a wicked thing to say.'

'But it's true, isn't it?'

Curbing a sharp desire to slap her, Merynne said coldly, 'Mr Wellan's affairs and mine aren't yours. And remember he isn't your father until I marry him, next week.'

Bethany said no more but Merynne could sense the scornful unchildlike knowledge beneath the innocent facade. For the first time she viewed the prospect of becoming Mrs Wellan with relief. Then, at least, she'd be in a position to point out the rebellious influence the colourful housekeeper was wielding over their daughter.

8

The wedding took place quietly at Penjust on a day when the surrounding moorland hills were shrouded in thin rain. Everything appeared grey – as grey as Merynne's thick velvet cape and bonnet – except for Bethany who for the occasion had been bought a blue fur-trimmed outfit that emphasised the glow of her rosy cheeks, brilliant eyes, and dark glossy curls.

Merynne had been dubious about having her there, expecting at least some unpreditable outburst that might embarrass the proceedings. Frank, however, had insisted and the little girl had behaved with quite surprising elegance, as though she was some high-born princess in attendance.

Wellan was amused, but Merynne was too emotionally bewildered to feel anything except that she was in some sort of dream. Nothing seemed completely real. Here she was – going through a wedding ceremony with someone she'd been married to before, but who now seemed almost a stranger.

On the way to the town, feeling a male hand touch hers reassuringly at intervals, she'd experienced intuitively the old familiar feeling of excitement – of electrical contact – that Nat's touch had given her in the past. But whenever she stole a glance at him the sensation was replaced by shock and brief unbelief. Although in some ways he was so like the young man she'd known in the far-off days before she'd married Will Drake, in others this more mature, broad, smartly-clad figure wearing the tall felt hat above the strongly carved features – represented a completely different personality. The up-turned brim was slightly tilted forward in the manner of fashion, emphasising the dark side-burns, and jut of chin protruding from the high winged collar. The tailed black velvet coat was waisted and cut away from the front. He also had a cape styled in the fashion set by the Italian opera *Courier des Dames*, which he'd loosened at the neck for the journey.

Once more, noting such details, Merynne was completely bemused. One thing alone was clear. Nat Herne – or Frank Wellan as he had now become – had again spun his magnetic web about her, and won. She didn't even recall having agreed, in words, to re-wed him. He'd somehow forced her – mainly through Bethany – into silent acceptance.

But had she ever really wanted to refuse?

Firmly she managed to set her mind against answering.

*

The ceremony was brief and attended by only two witnesses – casual acquaintances of Frank's, who had never before seen or heard of Merynne Drake. Immediately afterwards, the couple, with Bethany between them, drove to a coaching house, The Golden Goose, where they had refreshments and wine. Then they started off again for Morningsgate. At a point high up on the moors Wellan told the driver to stop the chaise. The vehicle drew up with a rattle.

'But why?' Merynne queried, staring in bewilderment at the wild expanse of hills under the misty rain driven sky.

The light was fading, and the pale glimmer of an oil lamp streaked across the road from the door of a huddled low-roofed hostelry. Her husband took her arm. 'I want you to meet some of the tenants, and present my daughter.'

She drew away. '*No*. You can't do that. It wouldn't be fair –'

Not looking down at her, he answered quietly but firmly, 'Don't argue, love, "Miss Bethany Drake" I shall say, "who becomes Bethany Wellan".'

Bethany clapped her hands. 'Yes, yes. Then you'll be my real Pa for ever.'

Chagrinned, Merynne made no further comment. She allowed herself, coldly, to be helped from the carriage, and with Wellan's hand on her free arm was guided across the lane towards the door of the squat building. Bethany, for once, was silent, a little awed, and certainly fascinated by her surroundings which held, for her, the mystery of a fairy-tale. 'Like going into a magic cave', she thought, and her small hand tightened instinctively in Wellan's. Presently he moved ahead.

All around them the gnarled twisted branches of leafless trees and bushes seemed to wave and beckon with the grotesque semblance of witch-like creatures of another world. Ahead of the inn, the gaunt dark shape of an abandoned engine-house stood with black holes of eyes watching. There were great boulders looming beast-like from clumps of thorn, heather and gorse, always the damp air swirling in coils of mist, giving the impression of constant movement to the scene. During those few seconds of leaving the chaise and reaching the hostelry, Bethany's imagination was set alight. She recalled Vonny's tales of William Shakespeare – of *The Tempest* in particular, Ferdinand, Ariel and the ugly Caliban. Oh it all seemed true for that brief space of time. She was the lovely Miranda, daughter of Prospero, king of an enchanted world where dreams and fancies were more real than practical everyday life.

When she lifted her chin up with the damp air on her young lips smelling of earth, undergrowth, and faint tang of the sea, she was filled with a rush of excitement. She wanted to prance over the stones away – away – far into the unknown world that beckoned.

Then she heard her mother saying, 'Bethany dear, straighten your bonnet. Here –'

Merynne bent down, wiped stray curls from the young forehead, and slightly adjusted the strings.

The dream faded.

Bethany gave a short jerk of impatience before going on obediently along the thread of light zig-zagging from a chink of open doorway. A bulky male figure staggered out, moving uncertainly down the path. Wellan stood aside with Merynne and Bethany until the man – obviously a sailor smelling strongly of liquor – had passed. Then they entered the hostelry, and Bethany was once more astonished. Lamps were swaying, and a number of customers, mostly men, were gathered round the bar. At a small table near the rosy glow of a log fire, a bearded stout-bellied individual wearing a fisherman's cap, had his arm round a red-headed woman whose dress had fallen off one shoulder revealing a plump white breast.

'Look, Mama – look at that,' Bethany cried, pointing and giggling. Merynne glanced at her husband defiantly. 'Nat – *Frank*,' she corrected herself quickly. 'This isn't the place for a child.'

'Oh, it'll do her no harm,' Frank remarked casually, 'not like the lonely walks she took at Tarnefell.'

He was guiding them to a table in an alcove when the bearded man suddenly began to sing. He had a good resonant voice, and the melody was Celtic – either Cornish or Irish – a wild merry tune that set others joining in. The red-headed woman was pulled to her feet and with the man's arm round her waist, started swaying to the rhythm. The song rose and fell resonantly, telling of untamed far-off places, of mountains and rivers, and turbulent seas – of passion and love, and deep despair – most of all of the lusty joy of living.

The atmosphere became magnetised with longing, so highly charged that Bethany could no longer contain

herself. In a flash she'd broken away from Frank and
Merynne and was dancing near the merry couple, rosy lips
wide in laughter, eyes bright, curls flying, as her small feet
tapped and her lissom young body pirouetted and sprang,
quick as lightening, over the flagged floor. Merynne called
and would have rushed to capture the child, but Frank
restrained her. Men with mugs in their hands moved away to
leave a clear space. Other voices died. Only the man still
sang, his voice in harmony with the leaping logs and flying
shadows – with the small prancing figure, whose childlike
beauty and vitality filled even those bemused by rum and
gin, into quiet wonderment.

At last it was over.

The singer, swaying a little, returned to his stool, followed
by the red-headed woman. Frank strode into the middle of
the scene and captured his young daughter, leaving her
bonnet lying on the floor. From silence there was a sudden
roar of applause, of shouting for more. But Bethany, shy
following her outburst, hid her face against her father's
strong chest.

He was grinning, sensing already that this child of his own
flesh could one day make a name for herself – and that he'd
see she had no trouble in doing so. He'd watch and care for
her in every way possible, not only because he'd bred her,
but because she was also Merynne's.

When he'd ordered wine and refreshment he glanced at
his wife tentatively. Her cheeks were flushed; she looked
very lovely.

'There's nothing to worry about,' he told her quietly.
'Our daughter's one in a million. She'll make her mark.
You'll see.'

'In what way?' Merynne's voice was sad. 'In this kind of
place? Making a spectacle of herself?'

'No. Not in this kind of place. I've a hunch she'll tread the
boards of the world. I've the money to back her. It'll be her
choice anyhow.'

His eyes strayed fondly over the little girl's face. She was already half asleep on his knee.

'You don't know what you're doing,' Merynne told him. 'You haven't the first idea of her nature.'

'Ah, but I have – and yours too.' His voice became husky, intimate. 'And tonight I'll prove it to you, my love,' he continued, 'what we once had will be nothing to what we'll discover from now on.'

It was being unduly optimistic, but he wasn't aware of it.

What Frank Wellan, alias Nat Herne, wished for, he certainly got – eventually, and just then he saw no reason for the pattern to be discontinued or changed in any way.

*

She was seated at the dressing table brushing her long mane of shining hair when he entered the large bedroom at Morningsgate later following a meal in the dining room. Her arm moved easily in slow rhythmical strokes, betraying none of the tension she felt. He came softly up behind her; the hairbrush fell to the floor as his two hands encased her breasts from behind. The contact and pressure of his touch against her skin sent a shiver of trembling through her. She half turned her head towards him. Lamplight lit the curve of her rounded slim neck, giving a satin sheen to the line of jaw and skin. His lips gently brushed her shoulder, travelling downwards then up again until they found the moist sweetness of her own. With hands that shook slightly he untied the ribbons at her throat, and drew the lace-trimmed lawn garment from her body, leaving the naked curves of stomach and breasts white as sculpted ivory washed to a pale gold glow. Purposefully he lifted her up. Gently his mouth sought the silky triangle of hair between her thighs, and almost reverently he kissed it. Her two hands reached to him in passion, as his nightshirt fell away and they were naked together, lit to fire and beauty by unquenchable desire.

He carried her to the bed. Any bitterness there'd been or

sexual antagonism of the past was swept away by the ecstasy of mutual need.

'You are my love,' he whispered, 'my woman – my own – come – come –'

In a tide of passion they were united as one flesh.

When all was over he eased himself briefly above her, and stared deep into her eyes. She smiled; her pulse quietened, leaving only the magic of wonder and delight about her. Then, suddenly, he sprang from her, light as a panther, and said, 'Heavens! I forgot to look in on Bethany, and I told that woman I would.'

He reached for his wrap. Disillusionment, like a heavy stone, deadened her heart and spirit.

'Bethany!' she echoed dully. 'Oh yes, of course. Bethany.'

Unaware of the feminine hurt – the subtle jealousy in the short remark, he went to the door, saying, 'Try and rest, I'll not be long. But I must take a look in at the study. There's a paper I have to get off in the morning.'

Her daughter. Papers. Business. Resentment flooded her, because she should still be lying in his arms. It was as though love, on his part, had suddenly become superfluous – a pleasurable taste of lust to be shrugged off lightly once experienced.

And for this she briefly hated him.

9

It was unfortunate that following Merynne's first night with Frank at Morningsgate, business continued to interfere with their relationship. The mining captain of Wheal Chace arrived with the unsettling news of a landslide joining the new shaft which would cause considerable delay, and also that an engineer, contrary to previous expectations, feared the yield of ore could be less than expected.

Wellan was taken aback. 'What do you mean, *less?*' he demanded. 'I had two qualified opinions. What the devil's the use of getting the best men in the country to make a survey if they can't even judge whether the project's worthwhile or not? I've put a damned lot of cash and energy into this venture and given a promise to many families out of work they'll soon be earning pay again –' He broke off when the wooden expression on Joe Varney's, the captain's, face, didn't change. 'Well?' Frank persisted. 'What about it?'

Varney shrugged. 'That's the way of things sometimes, surr,' he said. 'You can never be a hundred per cent sure of copper and tin. If there's something there waiting to be worked, the mine'll carry on all right, given no more bad luck. But as for the future –' he broke off continuing doubtfully, 'I'm not happy about that. An' you had a talk with Mister Robbins he'd be able to explain better'n me.'

Wellan turned away abruptly, his face grim. 'Is he at Wheal Chace now?'

'Yes. If you remember, you said you'd be there a bit later.'

During the excitement of wedding arrangements Frank had forgotten.

'All right. Go back now. I'll start off as soon as possible.'

It was already eleven o'clock, and after a lazy breakfast in bed Merynne was only just dressing. She'd look forward to a day with her husband. After his passionate love-making of the night and his sudden departure from the marital bed, she'd hoped for renewed attention and some show of affection. She was only half dressed when he entered the room, and was seated on the bed with a negligee round her shoulders, pulling on a silk stocking. Her hair was loose, giving her the brief impression of some shy nymph preparing to meet her lover for the first time. So Dégas might have painted her. She glanced up quickly, a rose-glow deepening in her cheeks.

'I'm sorry, love,' Frank said in practical tones. 'I've got to take off now – trouble at the mine. Calculations wrong, I guess.'

'You said we might go to Truro –' she reminded him, disappointment and irritation sharpening her voice.

'I know, I know. Some other time. An outing can wait. This can't. Anyway you've plenty to do –'

'What?' the word held the impact of a pistol shot.

He looked annoyed.

'How the devil do I know? You're a woman; women can generally occupy themselves some way –'

'Oh yes. Of course they can.'

'Now look here, Merynne, there's no need to be uppity. You weren't a nagger in the past.'

'The past was different.'

'It certainly was.'

He came to her quickly, put both hands on her shoulders, and kissed her on both cheeks. Not passionately, but dutifully, as from habit.

'Oh, very well. You'd better not waste time,' she remarked, turning away.

He sighed with relief.

'That's a good girl, love. We'll make up for things later.

Plymouth might be a better idea than Truro, anyway. I've a man to see there, and we could kill two birds with one stone.'

She didn't reply, and after a moment he was gone.

Downstairs Bethany was with Vonny, following her about in various household tasks. Merynne, who was still irritated, but was beginning to resign herself to the child's infatuation for the colourful housekeeper, finished dressing, pulled on her boots and cape, and went out for a walk.

It was quite by chance that when Madame Duvonne, helped by Bethany, was arranging the flowers, the kitchen girl, May, arrived at the conservatory to say that someone, '– A mos' colourful gentleman, Maister Toby Finch, was at the side door, wantin' to see an old friend of his – Laurette, he did say, ma'am,' the girl continued breathlessly, 'madame.'

For some seconds Mrs Duvonne simply stared, then with both arms extended, she exclaimed excitedly, 'Toby, did you say, really *Toby*? Toby Finch?'

'Yes, ma'am. No mistake.'

Without another word, cheeks glowing, eyes bright with excitement, and a few dark locks broken from their combs, the housekeeper rushed by, down the hall, looking ten or more years younger. Bethany followed. She was in time to see, from the kitchen door, her adored Vonny fling herself into the arms of the most odd and colourful-looking gentleman. He wore a red spotted neckscarf, tied in a floppy bow dangling over a shabby green velvet jacket which was patched on one thigh. Yellow breeches that had seen better days were tucked into heavy boots. The pattern of his waistcoat was faded. Ginger curls parted in the middle, framed a cheerful middleaged face, and on one pink cheek he wore a patch.

'Oh, Laurette, m'dear,' he was saying between mutual gasps of affection and welcome, ''tis glad I am to see you. Travellin' all the country I've bin these many years – "Finch the singer" one night, "Toby the Tumbler" the next. Those were the good times mind you. There were worse – but what could you expect of an old player like me, eh? An' one with his company gone, an' Mr Gaylord away on his own –?' He laughed at the woman forced herself from his arms and made him sit on a bench by the fire.

'You must have something hot to drink and eat,' she told him, 'then we can have the full story. I've wondered about you so often – you and Mr Gaylord.'

He nodded. 'And me. I've seen him though.'

She put a tankard on the table with a rattle. 'You *what*? You have really?'

He nodded, reaching both of his large hands to the blazing logs. 'Quite by chance, in a tavern near Bodmin. Bin roamin' Europe – made quite a good living for hisself, so I heard. An' now, would you believe it? He's a mind for startin' all over again.'

'What do you mean, Toby?'

'He's got *plans*, darlin', for havin' another theatre; so we could be in luck again.'

'But –' She stopped what she was doing, and rushed back to him. '*Where*, Toby? And how? Has he the money?'

'Ah, that's the snag. Not enough. But if he gets the chance – you mark my words, Laurette, he'll get the stage all right in these parts, and mebbe Lunnon as well. I've a great faith in Gaylord Werne.'

'So have I,' Mrs Duvonne admitted, 'but without the means no one – even as brilliant as Gaylord can get far.' She moved to a cupboard, took food and a bottle from it, and placed them on the table. 'Now you come and have a bite, Toby, before we start gossiping too much. There's so much I want to know – about you, and any others of the old company, if you've heard anything.'

He got up and settled himself at the table. 'No, there's nothing to talk of the others,' he admitted, 'not that I've heard anyway. But –' his voice changed denoting the comical intonation of a gentleman's, 'am I not sufficient for thy lovely eyes, madame?'

'Come now, Toby. None of your compliments, except to eat my food and drink this good mead.'

Toby, obligingly for himself and for her, started immediately. All through the short discussion, Bethany had been watching, fascinated, half behind the door. Suddenly she could contain herself no longer. She stepped boldly into the kitchen and stood looking up at Toby.

'Hello, Mr Finch,' she said.

His eyebrows shot up above his pink cheeks. He regarded the small figure in amused surprise.

'Who's this then? A princess?'

Her laughter tinkled with the quality of silver bells. 'No I'm not. But I'd like to be, because princesses dance, don't they? And I do too. Last night I danced. Just like this –'

She lifted her arms and twizzled round.

'That's fine,' Toby said. 'Better than any princess I'll be bound.'

'I can sing too –'

'Now, Bethany,' Laurette said firmly, 'You must be quiet and let Mr Finch have something to eat – he's come a very long way to see me – or I shall have to send you away.'

'Oh.' The little girl looked crestfallen, and dropped her head. 'All right.'

She went to the fireside and seated herself demurely on a stool.

Presently, well fortified by lammy pie, apple tart, cheese, and a liberal quantity of the excellent mead, Toby left the table and seated himself by the child. Following a large belch which made Bethany laugh, he patted his stomach and said, 'Pardon me, princess, 'tis a habit we players have when we're pleased. Now –' he leaned forward, making her think how much like a large rosy apple his face was – except of course, apples didn't have ginger hair – '– are you aiming to tread the boards like Mrs Siddons, miss, or kick a heel all covered in spangles and lace – an actress or dancer? Eh?'

'Now, Toby,' Madame Duvonne began reprovingly, 'don't put such wild ideas into her young head. She has enough already. And I'm quite happy here. Good places are hard to find, remember, it's my business to see no disrupting influence interferes in the household. I'm afraid Mrs Wellan, Bethany's mother, wouldn't approve of such talk.'

'And since when did you so take note of any other woman's opinion, darlin'?'

'Since I had to,' came the direct answer. 'When the curtain fell on our last act.'

'Ah! but it can rise again,' the man said with a significant wink and wag of the fingers. 'Gaylord, our Mr Werne, as I've just said – has a mind to make a come-back with a flourish. That theatre I was tellin' you of – he's got one in view already. The Ring Theatre in Redlake, it's up for sale; they went all wrong there in the last few years according to him – too much heavy stuff put on. Folk don't always want Shakespeare – they want a change o' moods – a bit o' melodrama, then comedy, filled with a turn or two of song or acrobatics. *Variety*! that's what's needed these days, somethin' to cheer folk up – specially hereabouts with mines closing, an' the gentry gettin' worried an' bored. Oh make no mistake about it, Gaylord's got his finger on the spot.'

'With no money to make anything come true. And talent? What about that?'

'Both'll come in due course if we all watch out and grab any chance there is.'

'We?'

He grinned.

'You'n Gaylord an' me. An' mebbe –' his eyes slid to the wildly excited Bethany '– this young lady. She's got talent I'd swear my life on it. She could be the toast –'

At that precise moment the door from the hall opened, and Merynne walked in.

She tried not to show disapproval, but Laurette sensed it, and explained placatingly, before Merynne had a chance to criticize, 'This is a friend of mine, madam – Mrs Wellan. – Finch, Mr Toby Finch.'

Toby got up with a flourish, and with his hand on his heart, bowed before the elegant young figure, and said ingratiatingly, 'Your servant, ma'am.'

He'd have taken her slim hand, but Merynne drew back.

'How do you do, Mr Finch.'

He lifted his head, stared at her very directly, and it was then that her heart warmed very slightly to the tilted mouth and twinkling eyes. In his youth she guessed he could have broken many hearts.

Before other conversation could ensue, Bethany exclaimed excitedly, 'He's an *actor*, ma. He does things on the stage, like – like me, like dancing, and – and standing on his head. You *can* stand on your head, can't you, Mr Finch?'

'Ah well now,' he scratched one ear. 'There was a time when I could roar like a lion, climb like a monkey, squawk like a parrot, and even put me big toe in me mouth if I wanted to. But when a son-of-a-gun reaches my years he has to turn to other things.'

Bethany, who had been smiling, suddenly sobered, 'Why do you call yourself a "son-of-gun", Mr Finch?' she enquired.

'Because I was once in the army, me dear. But that was before –'

'Toby,' Mrs Duvonne interrupted, 'Mrs Wellan is waiting for Miss Bethany.' She cast a fleeting glance at Merynne, 'I'm so sorry, ma'am. This visit was quite unexpected.'

'I understand,' Merynne replied noncommittally. She reached for her child's hand and took it.

'Come along, darling.'

Very reluctantly, Bethany was led away by mother.

Toby Finch left Morningsgate a little later, after informing Laurette that he might be returning shortly. 'I've a meeting with Mr Gaylord,' he said, giving a characteristic wink. 'There's somethin' churnin' in me head that says findin' you's been opportune – most opportune.'

'And *how* did you find me, Toby?'

'Ah!' Again the characteristic trick of his nose. 'A little pedlar fellow by name of Tom Goyne called in at a certain kiddleywink when I was partaking of me refreshment –' another wink, 'and after I'd described your charms my dear, most aptly, he said, "And her name is Duvonne you say? Sure I know the lady. Along there, past the stream and to the left; lavish place, bought by a racy rich customer called Wellan," – so off I went and here I came. And here, if I'm not mistaken, there'll soon be Mr Gaylord also.'

'Toby, what are you up to?'

'You'll know soon enough, darlin', soon enough.'

A minute later he was striding away over the moor.

The housekeeper, although slightly puzzled by Toby's overt references to Gaylord Werne, had nevertheless a shrewd idea that they concerned finance and the possibility of Mr Werne acquiring Redlake's Ring Theatre. The idea stimulated her. Admittedly, Toby Finch was given to wild plans at times, but if Gaylord Werne set his heart on a project it was generally a feasible one that handled properly could be successful.

In this case she felt certain – indeed Toby had admitted it – that money was the problem. Frank Wellan had it. Was that the answer? It appeared so simple. But during the brief time she'd been Wellan's housekeeper Mrs Duvonne had learned he could be shrewd and close-fisted when necessary. He certainly wouldn't buy a pig-in-a-poke or be induced to squander any part of his fortune on a wild-cat scheme with no sure dividends to offer.

Could Gaylord give that surety?

For a week following Toby Finch's visit she ruminated over the subject, eventually deciding that Toby had merely conceived the idea, and then put it aside. Probably Gaylord himself had decided to consider it.

In this she was wrong.

On a fine winter's day of rough winds and wild seas, Mr Werne himself arrived at Morningsgate, for a 'business' talk with Frank Wellan.

10

Toby Finch's visit to Morningsgate resulted, through devious means on his part including a meeting with Gaylord Werne, in Frank Wellan agreeing to see Werne concerning the latter's business ambitions in the Ring Theatre.

Frank, already a little bored and frustrated by the mediocre progress and uncertain future of Wheal Chace was in need at that particular moment, of new stimulus and excitement. His existence, since marrying Merynne, had not in any way worked out to plan. His wife though dutiful and willing in bed, held something aloof from him which he could not fathom. Their first night together had been for the most part satisfactory – or so he'd believed. But passion had changed in her; it was as though she held something against him. Her expression at times was too watchful and faintly condemning. Yet what the devil had she to complain about? Surely she couldn't be still fretting over Will Drake's death?

Once, when she referred to the farm, he said, 'Time you stopped looking back isn't it? Or can't you get Drake out of your head?'

'Will?'

'Yes, *Will*. He's dead. But I'm alive – your true husband; so are you. We've everything going for us. We want each other. Then –'

'I know that. I don't mean to throw him back into your face. I don't *want* to remember him at all; not really – except that he's Luke's father. But the way he went –' she gave a little shudder. 'It wasn't like him; he was such a quiet reasoning man.'

'Meaning I suppose that you still reckon I could've given a shove or sent the bullet through his body?' His voice was hard, contemptuous, bitter.

'No.' The word came out shrilly. Two spots of flame burned in her high cheekbones. 'How could I have married you if I really – if I *really* doubted you Nat – *Frank*? How do you suppose –'

'I don't suppose anything. That's not my way. I see things clear and straight whether right or wrong. And to me it's obvious you don't trust me. Well – go on with it then. Don't expect me to be on my knees praying for you to believe me. One day maybe you'll see sense. Let's hope so. In the meantime keep your mournful thoughts to yourself and stop looking so damned high-and-mighty-holier than thou!'

Instantly she was on the defensive.

'Don't speak to me like that.'

'I'll speak to you as I like, madam. It's my privilege – so remember it and keep your pretty mouth shut.'

He strode away, annoyed with himself for having so crudely lost his temper and dignity over Will Drake – that stiff-necked farmer. Even to have been jealous of him – especially a dead man – was an affront to his pride. But Merynne should have learned to be more tactful and considerate of his feelings. He'd done enough for her and more than most men would in his position – sweated his guts out in blazing Africa in order to give her the best – played along with her when he'd returned and found she'd given herself to another man – all for the sake of her good name and that son of hers, Luke. Her good name! What a farce. As for Luke, he was a bastard, whichever way the law looked at it. Not that he bore the boy any grudge. He couldn't help it, poor little devil, and he, Frank Wellan, would see always that he was treated properly as a member of the Wellan family.

Everything could work out satisfactorily provided Merynne got the lingering image and suspicion concerning Drake's death out of her mind. In the meantime he'd this other project to consider – the matter of the Ring Theatre. Toby Finch had delivered the message personally – a well-groomed Finch who had needed all his undoubted acting ability to present himself as a 'gentleman' well up in the theatrical profession. His high opinion of Mr Gaylord Werne – of both his imaginative and practical abilities – had stimulated Frank to such an extent that he'd invited Gaylord to Morningsgate for a short stay.

Although not specifically stated, Wellan was under no illusion concerning the reason for the prospective meeting. Werne wanted 'backing' – to put it bluntly – money. Well – that was not assured. Frank was already used to requests of such a nature. Men with gold to invest generally were, and at the moment in spite of Wheal Chace's disappointing returns – he had plenty in his pocket. A little gamble – if it appeared justified, might pay off, and bring additional colour to his life. But he must be sure of his man, the pros and cons, and possibilities or otherwise of the venture. The old adage that a fool and his money were soon parted would never apply to him. He would go so far, if he felt like it, but no further.

Much would depend on his assessment of Gaylord's character. If the fellow had guts, was as brilliant as the nimble-tongued Toby Finch said, and if the future of a new, changed, Ring Theatre appeared promising – then, by Gad! he thought, with a stab of enthusiasm, he'd be prepared to sink a little capital into the scheme.

A wild dream? Maybe. But he'd always had more than a fair share of them himself. However, fortunes and success were not built from sitting placidly on one's backside in a haze of hesitation, but in getting down to solid facts and action. A little recklessness in the right direction could work wonders.

So when the true reason for Gaylord's visit drew near, Frank was already stimulated by a rising sense of exultation.

'I'm counting on you to use all your charm on this fellow – and your wits,' he told Merynne confidently.

'What do you mean, "my wits"?' she enquired coolly. 'I know nothing at all about actors or theatres.'

'Oh, but you've a cool head on you – when you feel like it,' he told her. 'Women are sometimes more shrewd in guessing whether a character's genuine or not. I want to see this fellow from every angle. Watch if he's likely to fall for feminine flattery, or if his head's screwed tight all round in the business direction. His name's got a funny sound to it; did you ever hear anything like it? *Could* be genuine I guess but I doubt it. On the other hand –' he broke off, shrugged, and added '– anyway whatever he likes to call himself is his own affair. A little self advertisement does no one any harm, I s'pose, and in the theatre could be an advantage. One thing's pretty sure – we can expect Mr Gaylord Werne to be a dandy in his way.'

Frank's prediction turned out to be only partly true. When, a few days later, the visitor arrived, he proved to be far less colourful in appearance than Toby Finch. For the occasion he had dressed meticulously but unobtrusively in light grey. He was small, slim, thin-featured, with grey thinning hair above an intelligent wide forehead. The eyes were grey also, shrewd and penetrating, under bristling bushy brows. His manner, though friendly, was precise and dignified. Wellan knew at once that he was in the presence of a man of ambition who knew his own mind, and would be fairly capable of judging those of others.

Mutual greetings were cordial. After a formal introduction to Merynne, Gaylord gave a brief slight bow, raised her hand to his lips lightly as though he were some courtier on a formal visit, and said, 'I'm delighted to meet you.' Then he turned his attention to Wellan, betraying none of the sharp interest he'd taken in the young wife. He never missed the 'magic quality' in any woman, and Merynne Wellan certain possessed it. He could visualise her protrayal in certain poignant episodes behind the footlights. Would she react favourably – be capable of conveying her natural qualities to an audience, or overdo them? Even be coy or shy? One could never tell until the crucial test. And then of course there'd be the husband to contend with – this rich Wellan prospector from whom he hoped to get the necessary backing.

Thoughts flashed like lightning through Gaylord's mind. Wellan, obviously, was a unique character and a restless one. Avid for life and notoriety as well as power. Advertisement of himself and achievements would probably titillate him enormously. If he could be induced seriously to delve into his pocket on behalf of The Ring Theatre, there could be an opening week with proceeds going to charity. This would strike a favourable impression in the district and further afield – especially should the lovely Merynne Wellan herself appear.

Frank, Gaylord decided, would support the latter proposition and probably persuade his wife to agree. If not, or if she turned out to be stubborn, he, Gaylord Werne, would accept her decision with understanding chivalry. There were other beautiful women in the world, and other schemes to set the public imagination alight.

Those other alternatives, luckily did not have to be considered, because at the meeting between the two men later in the library, Frank's enthusiasm was roused considerably, more quickly than Werne had dared to hope. In what he said he was at first wary, studying the pros and cons of costing, and possible proceeds under a guise of practical business interest. On one question he was determined to obtain a satisfactory and precise answer before committing himself in any way.

'How do *you* expect to make a success of The Ring when it's failed so dismally recently?' he asked bluntly.

Gaylord allowed a faint smile.

'Because I have my finger on the pulse of the theatre, sir, and a knowledge of what people want. I've travelled widely, absorbed the changing morals of human beings. Times at the moment are hard for many folk. For amusement, if they can afford it at all, they want something more light-hearted than the depressing blood and thunder and Shakespearian tragedy that The Ring has been putting on for years and years. They want charge, comedy, farce, with a mere smattering of sentimental melodrama. *Variety*, sir. That's the answer. Dance, song, sparkle, and romance. A touch of morality maybe, in certain turns – the ladies like a chance to shed a few tears between the laughter. Do you get me, sir?'

'Yes.' Wellan was quick to seize on the idea, and when the subject of Merynne's 'charity' appearance was mentioned, the flash of satisfaction on his face and brightening flash of his eyes told Gaylord he had won.

It was when matters had been more or less verbally settled that Frank called Merynne in. She was looking ethereally beautiful in soft grey velvet with a single rose at her bodice, and an edging of pink ribbon at her neck. Wellan smiled at his wife winningly.

'Come in, my love; Mr Werne and I have had an interesting talk, and he's made a proposition that concerns you.'

'*Me?*' she made an effort to smile, but a frown puckered her brows. What was Nat up to? – in her private thoughts he was always Nat – the wayward adventurer she'd first married, although she'd grown accustomed to calling, and hearing him called, Frank.

'Sit down, Merynne. You're sure to be interested.'
Before Wellan could do so, Gaylord, following a short bow, had placed a chair for her.

Bewildered, she seated herself. Mr Werne then started to explain. He had only spoken a few words when the door opened unexpectedly and a small figure rushed in. She was wearing a high-waisted blue dress, with a wide hem trimmed by dark ribbon. Her glossy curls were taken from her face by combs, but a stray curl had broken free as though the wind had brushed it. This was true. Unknown to her mother she'd run out of a side door to the back of the house and into the kitchen where Vonny was superintending the servants, to enquire about the visitor – the important Mr Gaylord Werne. The tips of her pointed small slippers were touched with dew; her cheeks glowed from excitement and fresh air, her expression was radiant. Life and vitality flowed from her.

Merynne sighed. 'Bethany –'

Bethany stopped, and drew a deep breath, 'Oh I'm sorry, Mama. I had to come. Vonny said – Vonny –'

'Yes?' Merynne's voice was severe. 'What did she say –?'

'Nothing really. I just wanted to see Mr – Mr Gaylord.'

'And why not indeed?' Werne said quickly. 'I'm enchanted to meet you. Quite enchanted.'

He got up, bowed low and brought the tiny hand to his lips. Merynne would have protested, but Frank stopped her. Bethany's smile was bright and radiant as sunshine.

'Are you a prince, Mr Gaylord?' she asked with her large luminous eyes staring admiringly.

'Well now – not exactly. Say perhaps – a maker of queens and princesses.'

'Princesses dance, don't they? So can I –' She whizzed round, laughing. 'How do you –'

'Now love,' Frank interrupted, 'not too many questions. Mr Gaylord and I have a lot to talk about, so run away for a bit, and you'll meet him again later.'

Reluctantly the child left.

There was a short pause during which Werne stroked his chin thoughtfully. It was broken by Merynne beginning apologetically, 'Please excuse her exuberance, Mr Werne. I'm afraid Bethany's always been –'

'Excuse? My dear lady!' There was a hint of irritation in Gaylord's voice. 'I'm grateful, most *grateful* to meet her.'

'But –'

'She has life, laughter, vitality and a rare quality that makes her a "natural". In short, your daughter, apart from her beauty, is a treasure, a find, Mrs Wellan.'

Frank glowed.

'I don't quite understand,' Merynne replied.

'Let me explain.' He was about to start, when Frank suggested they relax more, each with a glass of elder wine. He fetched a decanter from a cupboard, glasses and after a first sip and toast, Gaylord outlined what had been a sudden brain-wave, that not only Merynne should appear at the opening of The Ring, if it was posible for him to run the theatre, but her daughter Bethany as well.

'I have certain child songs and verses in mind,' he said, 'which would be ideal for her. She could become famous overnight –'

'Oh but –'

Gaylord lifted a hand. 'I know, I know,' he said, 'you don't want her spoiled. She wouldn't be. Her appearances would be for the *week only* – and all in a charitable cause. As yours would be.'

Merynne's cheeks reddened. 'I'm not an actress. I was brought up in a simple home. I –'

Frank's face darkened. 'My wife's too modest,' he interrupted abruptly. 'Please continue, Werne.'

Gaylord did so, stressing again the need for *variety* in entertainment, extolling the very different but equally alluring qualities of mother and daughter. Merynne, he pointed out, could provide an ethereal fey-like atmosphere in some 'Celtic twilight' episode, or in a sweetly sad dramatic item which would demand only a few words from her, whereas Bethany, for her contribution, would delight audiences by her natural capacities of *joie-de-vivre* and talent for dancing.

'I know,' he stated firmly. 'Spotting genius is my business. I have seldom made a mistake. Your young daughter could have a famous theatrical career before her if you wished it. But I know you don't. However – one little taste of success would do no harm. And –' with a significant glance at Frank

'– it could give The Ring a brilliant new start.'

The result of the meeting was that Wellan and Gaylord came to a financial understanding, which meant that The Ring Theatre would open the following March under the management of Gaylord Werne, with Merynne and Bethany both included in the cast for the first six days. It was stipulated by Frank that the charity to benefit should be on behalf of unemployed tin miners. Gaylord quickly agreed. Added glory for Frank Wellan meant further security for The Ring. Gaylord saw no cause for failure.

The future, indeed, looked very bright.

Merynne alone felt apprehensive, though she could not exactly have defined why.

Bethany was thrilled, and her adored Vonny gratified in knowing that, after all, her connections with the theatre were not over.

11

Frank had thought and hoped that Merynne would come to full agreement – even show certain enthusiasm for his new project. He was secretly aware that he had been reckless in his backing for Gaylord, but he believed it would pay off. As owner of a theatre that had once been well known – and was destined to be so again in the future – he could write off his disappointment over Wheal Chace as just one dull happening in an otherwise successful career. He wanted Merynne as a part of *his* new venture – his pride and ambition for her was a challenge that fired his imagination to excessive heights. The part Gaylord chose for her excerpt in the show was a tragic widow sorrowing for her lost love, which would provide a perfect vehicle for her grace and beauty; her dignity, sorrow, and longing would move an audience to tears. In contrast Bethany's vitality and inborn sense of humour, would immediately stamp her as a child of genius. He'd no intention of allowing either to continue in such a course. But to have their names famous was important to him. They would become legend throughout Cornwall; as the beautiful Merynne Wellan and Bethany – wife and daughter of Frank Wellan, his own popularity would be enhanced and his name remembered as benefactor to those in need.

Merynne unfortunately, didn't share his enthusiasm.

'You get such wild ideas, Frank,' she said one day, when he'd been discussing the new decor of The Ring. 'Everything has to be done in such a hurry. If you'd waited a little and considered, you might have seen things differently.'

'You mean you don't trust me?'

'Oh, I trust your intentions. But you haven't known Gaylord Werne long – do you really know him *now*? And Bethany –'

'What about Bethany?'

She sighed. 'She's already getting conceited. I know she's clever and attractive –'

'Unique.'

'Very well – *unique* – in her way. But it's not the way I wanted to see my daughter.'

'*Our* daughter,' he corrected her. 'In other words, you'd have preferred to have her forever confined in a schoolroom having to read and write and work on samplers, with her hair primly scraped back and wearing an apron.'

Her lips tightened. 'It would have been more sensible, and better for her.'

'That's your idea, not mine. It hasn't occurred to you, I suppose, that I might say the same about you?'

'What do you mean?'

'How much more fitting for a farm labourer's widow to be kept forever at the wash-tub or at the kitchen sink. It *could* have been like that you know.'

'Don't refer to me *or* to Will in that way,' she retorted hotly.

'I shall refer to Drake in any way I like if you persist in dragging up the past.'

'I didn't.'

'In your thoughts you did – in your stubborn refusal to face any new exciting challenge with me.'

She sighed.

'I didn't mean it to be like that. Oh, Nat – Frank –' her voice softened. 'Please believe me. I don't know where I am yet. The theatre – appearing on the stage! – it's like some ridiculous dream, a kind of strange nightmare –'

'Nightmare? Good God. Most women would give their eyes for the chance.'

'Yes. I suppose so.'

He slipped an arm round her waist. 'Darling – I know you better than you know yourself. Do you remember the day, long ago – before I went away – when I found you prancing round the Menan Stone, and you stopped and laughed, shaking your hair, and said you were dancing for the old gods –?'

She smiled slightly.

'Yes. I remember.'

'There was dew on your hair; the light caught it like diamonds and I thought – by heaven! that's what she shall have one day – diamonds and jewels galore. If I sweat my guts out somehow I'll dress my Merynne like a queen.'

She shook her head slowly.

'You're a strange mixture.'

The wonderment in her eyes embarrassed him, and embarrassment over *any* woman – even Merynne – was a new experience to Frank Wellan. He released her, and with an effort at lightness, said, 'I have my moods, but mostly I'm quite a tough guy.'

'Guy?'

'Oh just an expression I caught overseas – digging and clawing the ground for gold.'

'I see.' A touch of amusement twitched her lips. 'I'm glad at least that you're not attempting to blow up the Houses of Parliament.'

He relaxed then, laughed, and said, 'So I can take it you'll support me over this – the Theatre show?'

'You don't give me much choice,' she told him. 'Just so long as it's only for one week.'

Her acceptance was half-hearted, but when the practical business of the wardrobe arose, with Laurette advising, and once more devoting herself to stitching, pinning, snipping and bunching, her first grudge was replaced by growing enthusiasm. Where Bethany was concerned, Merynne still didn't approve; the child was so excited and exuberant and

– she had to admit – so talented and such a picture in her blue velvet outfit – she would be bound to have wide acclaim and praise. Frank had promised the period would only be for one short week. But Bethany had such a way of sweeping all before her, success might easily thwart his plan.

In the meantime, Laurette was delighted, and Gaylord, though wary of praise or congratulations before the result warranted it, was encouraging in his dry way.

'But don't think yourself a princess yet –' he told the little girl one day, following a rehearsal, 'just prancing about won't do; you've got to learn when to pause, smile and reach to the audience. Your curtsey at the moment, is a disgrace. Get your balance, my dear, and watch those wobbly knees.'

'Wobbly? But Mr Gaylord, I –'

'You heard what I said. Do as you're told, and you may even make a young queen in time.'

And Bethany smiled.

Life was going to be wonderful, just *wonderful*, she decided. Little she knew what was in store.

12

The first variety show at Redlake's Ring Theatre arrived. The exterior of the building which in a past age had been an old Town Hall, before a newer, better situation had been found for the latter, was brightly embossed in gold and red, half covered with placards and notices emphasising the brilliance of the artistes appearing, and the noble purpose of the inspired programme. The list was fully billed including such names as 'Pepita the Midget Princess', 'Carlos the Mighty Magician', 'The World Famous Singing Dogs', 'Toby Finch the Tumbler Comic', 'Kiki the Clown', an act from the heart-rending tragedy *The Forgotten Wife*, and several others. Heading all of them in glittering letters below Gaylord Werne's own name as producer, were the 'Lovely Merynne Wellan in an episode from the tragic drama *Forsaken but not Betrayed*', and just beneath it, but most conspicuously advertised – 'Bethany the Child Wonder', with a special appendage extolling her talent and great virtue in giving her services free.

Merynne, who in the end had done her best to fit the role intended for her, had been doubtful about the wording concerning her daughter.

'Isn't it a bit – vulgar?' she'd asked Frank. 'And won't it go to her head? I really do think that –'

Frank had silenced her by putting his hand to her lips.

'Sh, love, a little conceit for a week won't do her any harm. *Or* you –' And his look had so magnetised her she'd known there was no point in any further objection.

As expected, the hall that first night was packed.

Gentry as well as farmers, miners, and ordinary townsfolk attended.

Frank, magnificently attired in evening dress, had a central and most important seat in the circle from where he had an unimpeded view of the performance.

It had been arranged for Bethany to appear at the end of the first half of the show, with Merynne opening the second.

Vonny was in the wings to give both courage but to her surprise, Merynne found herself responding naturally to the excitement and stimulus. She knew she looked beautiful as the ethereal sad young wife and that Frank would approve. In the part she could play to him, give full reign to her emotions, and surely – *surely* then, the cloud would be dispelled between them for good. He would realise – he *must* – that however doubtful her thoughts concerning Will's death had been – nothing could ever come between Frank Wellan, her own Nat, and herself. Not even Bethany to whom he showed such abnormal devotion. Her heart warmed when she saw how lovely the child looked – how vital, sparkling, and full of joy. So like Frank.

'Your frock is so pretty, darling,' she said, taking the little girl's hand as her name was announced, before the parting of the curtains. 'You look –'

'Like a princess, Mama?'

'Yes, just like a princess.'

Moments later a tune had been struck up, and Bethany Wellan, an enchanted, inspired sprite – was curtseying, pirouetting, laughing, dancing and singing with the wild uncurtailed touch of genius that Gaylord Werne had recognised the first second he'd seen her.

She was more than a success – her performance was magical. Three times she was recalled to take prolonged applause. She lifted her arms wide as though to embrace the whole gathering, and everyone loved it. When at last the curtains were firmly closed for the interval, she was so breathless with excitement it was impossible for minutes to silence her.

'Yes, love, yes – you were beautiful,' Vonny assured her. 'But you must rest now. Sit down here, in my little cubby hole, while I attend to your mama. She has to have her hair arranged.'

Bethany pouted slightly. She didn't want to sit or rest. She didn't want the wonderful feeling of being admired and loved to end. She wanted to go on for ever – leaping and dancing and throwing kisses to all the world – especially to her father, who she'd known was watching her from the circle. Still, rather grudgingly, she obeyed Vonny – for the moment. While everyone was fussing over her mother surely he'd come and see her and tell her how proud of her he'd been.

The waiting seemed a very long time. She got up presently and wandered through the wings to a side door that opened on to the street.

The night was velvet dark, diamonded with tiny stars. Looking down towards the main thoroughfare the shapes of carriages and pedestrians passed with lanterns swaying, and the hollow sound of horses' hooves echoing over the cobbles. She had a sudden uncontrolled impulse to run the short way and see more closely what they looked like – the people of Redlake who travelled when it was night. Were they ladies with jewels in their hair, and tall-hatted men like her father? Or were some of them tinkers? Gipsies? The last thought filled her with awe, and a certain poignant longing. She remembered Rom and Thisbe and their children Tallan and Sheba, Bethany's friends who'd been drowned while they were gathering limpets.

A lump rose in her throat. How she'd have loved it if they could have been at the theatre that night to see her. But she might never meet them again, or even old Torgale who'd whispered magic to her as the winds moaned round Tarnefell. When she reached the corner of the street joining the main road, she was already half dreaming and feeling the natural reaction of exhaustion. And when a harsh old voice whispered in her ear, 'Lost, are ye, dearie?' she wasn't really shocked or frightened, just mildly surprised. She glanced up and shook her head mutely.

The face staring down at her through the fitful light and shade was bony, strong-featured, with grey locks straggling beneath a black shawl. Bethany would have turned and run back to the theatre, but at her first movement a hard hand gripped her wrist. The old face came closer.

'No need to be frit, darlin'. Not of old Jetta. You come with me darlin' an' I'll show 'ee all the magic o' the world –'

The little girl screamed, but her scream was lost in all the others sounds of the night – the clatter of cabs and horses and drunken laughter from a public house. The large hand swiftly covered the small face, smothering protest. Bethany felt herself lifted up with something dark and thick over her mouth.

'You just kip y'r mouth shut,' the coarse voice muttered. 'A good fairy I c'n be, when I feels like it – d'ye hear –?'

Bethany's feet struck out. Her kicks were useless. There was a sharp stab in her arm, a little gasp, then nothing but the night closing in, and feet padding through a side alley. A straggling drunk or two weaved from side to side taking no notice of the bent lurching figure on its own dark purpose with what could have been a sack of potatoes, or bundle of rags-and-bones slung over one shoulder. Five minutes later the child was bundled into an itinerants' van bound for the North. The company consisted of nomads of mixed blood – not true gipsies, but wily vagabonds with the knack of living as easily as they could – sometimes very comfortably – through the naivety of respectable folk. Begging, performing and stealing were part of their trade. They possessed nimble tongues and quick wits, and had very rarely been caught out. True Romanies such as Thisbe and Rom despised them, but as 'travellers' occasionally had contact.

When old Jetta placed the unconscious Bethany in the larger of the vans belonging to her son Wode and his wife Cora, her evil smile was triumphant.

'Good bargaining stuff,' she said, pulling the shawl from the little girl's face, 'a real beauty.'

Cora's lined good-looking face darkened.

'It's dangerous taking a young un of her kind. Pitch 'er out. They'll get on to us sure enough –'

The man spoke. He was bearded, swarthy, with an assessing gleam in his shrewd eyes.

'You leave 'er be. We'll tek care o' that. When she wakes there'll be a bit o' workin' on 'er to do. No one'll know 'er if you do your work proper, Cora.'

Jetta nodded. 'That's right. A fine boy she c'ld be, with them curls cut, and the hair made yeller.'

Cora shook her head. 'It's not safe.'

The man brought his hand smartly across her face. 'You heard what she said. My old woman knows. Now you get goin' with your washbasin, an' no more arguin' or I'll have the hide off y'r back.'

Grumbling, the woman felt her smarting cheek. 'And do you think the kid'll keep quiet?'

'She will. We'll bribe 'er first – try the little princess business – an' if that won't work we'll beat the guts out of 'er.'

So it was that by morning the ruthless group had moved towards Devon, with a fair boy in their midst. They called him Joe, and he appeared to be dumb. After the bleaching and a plate of broth, he showed no reaction whatever to their commands except to obey. There'd been no cause to placate or threaten. The drug had been more overpowering and potent than old Jetta had believed.

No matter. It was all for the best, members of the group decided; if the kid never recovered she'd be a godsend for begging purposes – with that lost innocent look on her. She'd have to be tried out of course – no use taking risks in the near future. But one day – well, one day maybe 'young Joe' would be decked out as a girl again, and sold at some great port where ships sailed daily for foreign places. Rich oil merchants and Arab princes were always eager for tender virgins. So it was their business to see she remained so.

Dawn brought sunlight to the spring day.

But Morningsgate was enshrouded in shadow and despair.

Gaylord Werne and Wellan had done their best to inspire hope into Merynne's heart, but only a sense of doom registered.

Bethany was gone. And it was Frank's fault.

*

'It's *your* fault,' was Merynne's constant accusation to Frank during the days that followed. 'If you hadn't insisted on this stupid acting business – and just for your own vanity too – just for that – Bethany would be with us now. We'll probably never see her again. Do you hear? – Do you *hear*?'

Her voice each time had been shrill and bitter, her face white with despair.

For two days Wellan had been patient and tried to reason. Enquiries were afoot, he said, all authorities had been informed and an extensive search was in process. Vehicles were being checked at certain points, so far with no success. But the truth was probably that the little girl had wandered off on her own and was hiding. They'd find her, she'd turn up.

'Why *should* she?' Merynne had demanded. 'She's been kidnapped, unless she's dead –'

On and on the tirade went. By the time Wednesday arrived Frank's mood changed.

'Tonight you're going to appear at the theatre as planned,' he told her grimly. 'The whole show's suffering. There's word getting about that The Ring is cursed, and folk are keeping away. You'll do your act tonight, Merynne, and do it well, or I'll know the reason why. I've sunk capital into this venture, and I don't aim to lose it all.'

'No, you wouldn't, of course not. Money always comes first with Nat Herne – money and adventure – always has and always will, – even before the life of our child –'

His eyes blazed. She knew she had gone too far.

'You say that once more, madam, and I'll teach you a lesson you'll never forget. So remember. And don't you ever – *ever* – accuse me of not caring for Bethany. Right along it's you who've been the cold one – letting her stray around Tarnefell, always on at her, scolding and disciplining – maybe if you'd been a little gentler with her, more of a real mother she wouldn't've taken any chance there was of escaping and turning to other folk –'

'Like your precious Vonny!' she could have bitten her tongue out for the revealing jealous remark.

'Yes, like Vonny,' he said harshly. '*Bethany*'s Vonny. Not mine.'

She gave a short contemptuous little laugh and turned away. In one gesture he caught her and swung her round. 'See you're prepared for the show tonight,' he said. 'I'll have a meal sent up here to the bedroom. If you're not ready at the proper time to go to the theatre, I'll dress you myself. And don't blame me if your face stings.'

He strode out, slamming the door behind him. There was the rattle of a key turning. She tried the knob, and found it was locked.

That evening, for the first time, 'Merynne Wellan' appeared at The Ring in *Forsaken, but not Betrayed*.

13

Bethany lived in a kind of half dream. She was not positively unhappy. The travellers saw to that. Kindness was shown to her, because the 'medicine' they gave her daily kept her acquiescent, and she liked being called 'princess' at night before being put to bed in a large box-like thing well padded with cushions. It was a kind of chest made by a seaman. The lid was always open, except when nosy strangers came poking around, and she liked watching the shadows play round the walls of the van, imagining them to be her servants, like those of queens in fairy-tales.

She knew something was wrong, but she couldn't remember exactly what, and when she was told that she'd been rescued from a wicked thief, she tried to believe it. In better, clearer moments, she didn't – quite. There'd once been someone so nice in her life – a handsome man that she'd loved and called 'papa'.

'Where is he?' she asked the black haired woman who brought her broth and made her wear the boy's clothes. 'Where's my pa?'

'You haven' got one dearie,' the woman told her. 'We're your family, an' you just remember it. Your name's Joe, an' you belong to us.'

'I don't. I'm not Joe. I'm –'

'Shh! you do as you're told or it'll be bad for you. Y'hear?'

When she continued to protest she was slapped once, then cuddled and given a large dose of the medicine. After that she forgot all about Frank and was quite content to be a princess at night, and a boy called Joe in the mornings.

The vans were stopped occasionally by the police. 'And who's this then?' a man in uniform enquired on one occasion.

'My son,' the hard-faced woman said defiantly. 'You ask 'im 'is name.'

'Well, lad? Tell me. What are you called?'

'Joe,' came the prompt reply, though the name was spoken in a whisper, almost as though he dare hardly say it. 'I'm Joe. That's me.'

The large eyes under the thatch of tow-coloured hair were quite innocent of guile. There was something puzzling about him, but the officer couldn't say what.

'He's a bit –' the woman touched her head significantly. 'Well, – reckon you can see f'r yourself. Not quite like the rest of us.'

'Hm.' After a further penetrating glance the man, mildly embarrassed, coughed, and turned away.

'We're looking for a young girl,' he explained, 'about the age of this little lad. If you hear of one wandering or in any kind of fix – anything suspicious, let us know, and you'll benefit. There's a good reward going.'

'*Reward?*' The bearded tinker appeared suddenly with a bundle of wood under one arm. 'How much then?'

The sum mentioned took him aback.

'All that for one little kid?'

'And more probably. The father's a rich man.'

'He must be. All right then. We'll keep out eyes and ears open, but tisn't likely our kind'll come across one o' them sort.'

March of that year, 1822, turned to April, bringing sweeter winds, blossoming hedgerows, and the speared budding heads of wild flowers to moors and fields. The earth smelled verdant from fine soft rain, and Bethany's health improved. The constant moving from one place to another, the feel of the breeze in her hair and being able to bathe in pools and streams of fresh water, gradually drove lingering fears from her mind. She needed less of the 'sleepy' medicine, and was excited when the begging process started, and she was allowed to accompany the tinker woman to doors of village cottages, and the home of small towns they passed through, selling bunched posies.

Being a boy could be fun; sometimes she was given a coin for 'the little lad to spend on sweeties'. The tinkers didn't let her keep it, but that didn't matter – they gave her something else instead – an extra piece of pie from a rabbit they'd poached on route, or a meat pasty. She began to enjoy wearing raggedy pants instead of dresses. When the vans stopped by the wayside for the night, she found trousers so easy to climb trees in. And her short hair didn't get tangled or caught by briars. Why it had to be washed so often and kept yellow, she couldn't understand, nor why she wasn't allowed to remember about the past. Actually, day by day, memory was beginning to register more clearly, although she didn't tell anyone. This was one of the things she'd learned – to keep her thoughts to herself. The travellers were always cross when they thought she knew more than she said.

'She's becoming one of us all right,' the man said to the woman one day, 'and I don't reckon she'll ever get her senses properly back again. Maybe it's safe now to let her hair go natural, an' get the skirts on her. Then we cu'ld get our hands on the reward.'

The woman threw him a sly watchful glance.

'Be careful,' she warned. 'If you ask me it's not time yet. Wait till summer's done an' she's no more use –'

The man grudgingly agreed. 'You could be right,' he said. 'Arter all, if she did start remembrin' – she cu'ld go tellin' on us, an' then we'd be in trouble. What's it for kidnappin', eh? Hangin', or transportin'?'

The woman scowled. 'There are times when I feel like cursin' y'r old woman for pickin' the kid up. Look at her now

– starin' wi' those great eyes. What's she thinkin' of? Sometimes I wonder –'

'Oh shut up. She's no wits to think at all, 'cept o' birds an' flowers an' messin' about in the streams. You ain't got nuthen to bother about on that score.'

But they were wrong.

They had a great deal.

Very gradually, in spite of drugs and the constant reminders of '– You're Joe you are – my boy and his, see? Joe! Joe. Just remember that.' A pattern was taking shape in the child's mind, and with it the subtle instinct that she mustn't reveal it. At first only small parts of the past registered – of Frank, her father, and a dark haired woman called Vonny who told her stories. Further back than this there was a funny faced stone, old Torgale, where she liked to skip and dance. There'd been another pa, too, and a baby.

She didn't know where they were now or how she'd got with the travelling people, and why she was a boy. Well, she wasn't really, and that was funny too. She wanted to ask, but daren't. Every time she opened her mouth to speak the travelling folk gave her a look that was frightening though she couldn't say why, so she held her tongue, and did what they said, knowing, deep down, that one day she'd remember. It was then that the 'pretending' period started. If she pretended not to know anything at all they didn't make her take so much medicine. She didn't sleep so much either. Why *should* she sleep in the daytime when the sun was shining and the winding lanes so lush with birds and flowers and small wild creatures? Visits to towns and villages could be exciting too. When ladies came to cottage doors and bought posies from the tinkers, they would often say, 'what a dear little boy', and buy an extra bunch for twice the money asked. It was like being in a play because by then she knew her real name was 'Bethany' though no one else did.

One person she couldn't bear was the old woman. The old woman was connected in her mind somehow with blackness and struggling, and not being able to breathe. She often dreamed about those dark things, but couldn't get any clear picture of what had happened.

Then, one evening when the woman took her into a wayside tavern to fetch a jug of ale, something happened that suddenly pierced her mind like a shutter clicking open from a window. As they were about to leave, a short bow-legged man appeared in the doorway. He wore a long green coat, and had a feather in his hat. Behind him, in the roadway was a pedlar's cart filled with an assortment of articles – medicine, toys, ribbons, yards of different materials, all manner of lucky charms and women's fancy beads. There were very few household goods that couldn't be produced at a cheap rate. There might be flaws in them, but they were usable, and had mostly been bought or bartered en route.

With a leap of her heart Bethany recognised him – not only because of his quaint attire, but because of the old donkey, Gyppo, waiting patiently by the cart. In the old days, at the farm, she'd given carrots to him, and once the funny man, Tom Goyne, had placed her on his back.

Yes, it was Tom Goyne.

Forgetting restraint or wisdom, the small figure in boy's clothes tore himself from the woman's grasp, spilling ale from the jug, and rushed outside.

'Gyppo,' Bethany called, 'it's Gyppo, Gyppo.'

Tom turned, staring. 'My dear life!' he muttered, 'if it isn't –' he bent down, '– is it you, lovie? Is it really Bethany Drake? – poor little child –' He could hardly believe his eyes. But he was a shrewd character not easily deceived by shorn bleached locks or a pair of ragged pants.

'Yes, it's me. It's me. But my pa's called Frank, and he – he –'

Her explanation was stopped abruptly by a fierce tug of the tinker woman's hand, while her other one covered the little girl's mouth. Bethany struggled. Terror filled her as she recalled the incident outside the theatre when the horrible old crone had dragged her forcefully away, half smothering her.

'You stop such talk!' she heard the woman saying harshly. 'The boy's my son, Joe – and a bit touched in the head. You kip y'r mouth shut mister, or there'll be trouble –'

'That there will!' The male voice of her husband emphasised. He'd come after his wife with a second jug. The day had been a profitable one on the roads. By then a little gang was already gathering, anxious to see a bit of fun or fight.

Tom glanced round warily, knowing he could do nothing by interference at that point. He'd be badly outnumbered, and even poor old Gyppo might suffer. The only sensible course was for the child to keep quiet while he managed to contact someone in authority. Bethany's disappearance had been the talk of the district. The priority now was to allay suspicion in the ugly cunning minds of the thieving tinkers so the poor little thing came to no harm.

He put a finger to his lips warningly, at the same time managing to nod his head and convey a message to the cowering child. She seemed to understand. A little of the fear receded from the enormous watchful eyes.

The pedlar gave a gesture of assent to the itinerants.

'Trouble?' he said, forcing a lop-sided grin. 'Who wants trouble? Not me. The old donkey and I's got enough as it is coverin' miles in the dusk, an' with a shaky wheel into the bargain. Tek no notice of the little lad. He's mistook me for someone else.'

He was going to his cart when the landlord called, 'An' doan' you want nuthen then? What about the rum, Tom? Not like you to miss your pick-me-up.'

Tom laughed, returned to the bar, winked and said, 'You'd better double it.'

'So it's like that is it? Who is she, Tom? Some fancy tart or a plump young chicken ripe for pluckin'?'

The room echoed with appreciative approval, and during the diversion the tinkers managed to escape with Bethany into the dark.

'An' don't you never talk like that again or you'll get a strap on your backside,' the woman said.

'An' more'n that,' the man promised.

It wasn't often they had to threaten but the child's recognition of Tom Goyne showed she was not half so 'dumb' as she looked, and for the first time since the kidnapping they knew real fear.

For the following few days Bethany was given more of the insidious medicine, while the two vans travelled ever northwards.

*

Meanwhile, confusion and discord mingled with heartache became a real threat not only to Merynne's marriage, but to the Ring Theatre.

After her second appearance on the stage, both Frank and Gaylord had to admit she was more of a liability than an asset. She recited her lines in a feelingless parrot fashion that 'boohs' and a negative reception from the audience didn't change. Her looks even seemed to have diminished. No 'make-up' could erase the lines of strain from her face or give allure to her slim figure. Her mind was far away with Bethany – she had no contact with the play or the crowd watching, and of course, they sensed it.

The other turns did their best, in their various items, to evoke interest and dispel lethargy, but it was as though a blight had fallen over the whole occasion.

The Ring was referred to as being cursed.

'It'll never get on its feet again,' one whispered to another. 'It's done.'

Gaylord was quite aware of the bleak reception, recognised also the full extent of harm superstitious talk could do. On the third day following the opening, he said to

Frank, 'Your wife will ruin everything. She's probably done it already. Keep her away, Wellan. I'll try and get Milly Peach from Exeter to fill the role. It's our only chance.'

And Frank glumly agreed.

*

April was a fine one spattered with primroses, violets, pale curling young bracken and brilliant splashes of gorse bright among the heathered hills. The garden of Morningsgate foamed with apple blossom and wild daffodils still blossomed in the tender green of thrusting grass.

In contrast the house seemed dark, without joy.

Merynne would have nothing to do with Frank, against whom she now held two grudges – Will's death and Bethany's disappearance. He was as worried as she was, but her concentrated bitterness and distress seemed to him unreasonable. He tried in every way he knew, to soften her, but any advances he made were repaid by a show of cold contempt or ice-cold fury.

Once, determined to end the humiliating situation he forced himself upon her when she was lying alone, after retiring for an early night.

She managed to free herself, scrambling from the bed, and clutching her nightdress to her chin.

Her eyes were cold slits of fury when she stood rigid and unyielding before him. He was shocked. 'What the deuce –?'

'Get out,' she said in very clear tones. 'Don't touch me. I don't want you. Can't you understand? It's all *your* fault – yours! – *yours.*'

'Oh, my God!' Suddenly weary of the melodrama, the constant vituperative refrain, he heaved himself up, pulled on his wrap, and went to the door.

'We'll talk later, madam,' he said, 'when you've recovered your senses.'

There was a snap of a latch clicking, followed by the echo of his footsteps down the corridor. Then, except for the sleepy chortle of birds outside, and the monotonous tick of the clock, silence.

Wearily Merynne returned to bed and lay there in complete exhaustion. Tears clouded her eyes, but did not fall. All she wanted from Frank was comfort – comfort and reassurance. Not only on account of Bethany, but because she had discovered only recently that she was to have another child.

It was unfortunate she hadn't told Wellan before he left her.

That night he got very drunk.

Laurette found him on the floor in his study. The air was thick with alcohol. There was a great bruise on his forehead where he'd fallen against the table.

She kneeled down, and stroked the damp hair from his forehead. He opened his eyes, staring at her in bemusement.

'No good,' he murmured. 'No bloody good. My fine – w – w – wife don' want me. A failure – that's what I am – no-one wants Nat. Poor ole Nat – no, Frank; that's me – Frank Wellan –' incoherently his voice wandered on.

Laurette eased an arm under his head. 'Yes, dear, yes I know what you meant –' she said, as though soothing a child. 'But you're wrong, you know. Everyone admires Mr Wellan –'

His eyes widened. 'You too – do you?'

'Of course.'

He reached towards her, one hand enclosing a breast.

'I want you,' he muttered. The smell of her thick hair was fragrant and sensuous brushing his face and enfolding him in a flood of desire.

'Lie with me –' he murmured. 'Lie with me. You're warm – loving –'

'Yes, dear, yes.'

Somehow she got him to her room. Sexually she desired him, but stronger even than the sex was the protective, motherly instinct to give him peace. And this she could do effectually. She knew men.

There was no sense of guilt or betrayal in her, and when all was over and he lay at peace by her side, gratitude filled her that once more she could have fulfilled what she had been for.

Merynne, for her, did not enter into the situation at all, and in the morning she and Frank could resume practical life in the normal everyday pattern. That night was just an incident.

14

When Frank woke in the morning following his night with Laurette, he was in his own single apartment reserved for late occasions when he didn't wish to disturb his wife. He was in night attire. Shirt, coat and breeches were neatly placed on a chair. Memory slowly returned. He looked round. There was no sign of Laurette. Somehow she must have got him there, though at this point he had no recollection how. At first he felt confused and uneasy. His head ached. He felt a brief sense of shame on Merynne's account, but this subsided as recent events registered. The betrayal and rejection had been on her side. The bitter words and hatred in her eyes had stung him more cruelly than he'd realised at the time. How she'd changed.

He'd still loved and passionately desired her up till then. Maybe he still did. But words could kill. A man like him needed a little softness and warmth in his life – and Laurette Duvonne had given it. As his senses revived, a glow of appeasement filled him, reviving the comfort of plump arms, satin skin, and sweep of thick silken hair. In a drift of cool air from the window, the fragrance of her body seemed to mingle with all the sweet summer earth smells of waking nature. There could be no future for them, of course. Even in his confused state he knew that. He was not a man prepared to deal with complex emotional situations. Merynne was his wife, and would remain so. In any event Laurette was pledged to her old role at The Ring. In a month's time she would have left Morningsgate. She would never again desert Gaylord or Toby Finch – neither would he wish her to. She'd go on with them as long as the Theatre continued, and heaven help them all if it didn't.

As he dressed, the headache eased a little, but with clarification of his thoughts, gloom descended and increased. The loss and problem of Bethany remained. There were still heavy expenses concerning the theatre to be faced. The mines were bringing in only the minimum of profit, and although Werne was still hopeful that the show could get off to a good second start, he was obviously doubtful.

Wellan could see the fortune he'd worked for already down the drain. He cursed himself for having sunk so much into the project. Indeed, the only bright spot in his life appeared to be Laurette, which could be only temporary.

She was coming up the hall when he went down to breakfast. Her faint smile was polite and friendly, but no more.

'It's a nice morning, Mr Wellan, sir,' she said as they passed. 'A light breakfast is in the small parlour. I thought you might not wish for a great deal to eat.'

He observed her closely. There was no hint of sarcasm in her voice, no faint touch of intimacy in her glance. They were back on the old terms of employer and employee, just as though nothing personal had occurred between them. Relief filled him. Merynne need know nothing about the brief affair.

His wife seemed nowhere about when he went to look for her later.

'She went out, surr,' he was told by a servant.

'Riding, do you mean?'

'No, surr. Just walkin'.'

'Which direction?'

'The moors at the back. T'wards that old mine, I think – the ruin. I did say it culd be dangerous, it looked like rain comin', but she took no notice. She looked kind of –'

'Yes?'

'Strained. Sort of far-away, surr.'

'I see.'

Without another word Frank strode away, put on a jacket, went to the stables, saddled a horse and took the track leading to the hills. What the servant had told him about approaching rain was quite true. Heavy massed clouds had already obscured earlier sunshine. The air was oppressive and sultry; no touch of wind stirred.

The bracken and late bluebells with clustered foxgloves, stood tall and motionless by boulders and standing stones. It was as though everything waited for a forthcoming explosion of the elements. Even the few sheep were already huddled against the stone wall of a small farm.

Wellan, now fully roused from his lethargy, kicked his horse to a smart gallop; at the first high ridge of the moors he halted, scanning the landscape. A quarter of a mile away the black ruin faced him like some evil spectre of the past guarding its own territory. The surrounding patch of scarred ground was considered not only completely sterile now, of ore, but dangerous. 'Bad land', the natives said. Frank himself was contemptuous of such superstition, but anxiety filled him as the first roll of thunder sounded from the west. Merynne had been in a strange mood since Bethany's disappearance. All sense of normal reasoning seemed to have deserted her. Towards him she no longer acted as a human being, but as a vehicle, merely, for blame and abuse – blame for their daughter's fate and Will's death. Fear of bogs or death down a shaft would not penetrate her obsessive search for the child. He knew she was in mortal danger.

He waited only a few moments with the bleak thoughts chasing his brain, then, at a cautious canter horse and rider went on again towards the stark landmark.

The first heavy spatters of rain fell. Once or twice he tunnelled his hands to his mouth and called, 'Merynne –

Merynne – d'you hear?' And again more loudly – '*Merynne –*' The sound was only a thin echo in the air.

Dark and unlovely, scarred with blackened patches of earth where moorland fires had been, the slopes stretched desolately under the inky sky. A thin breeze suddenly rose heralding the storm, shuddering through furze and heather with increasing force. The rain thickened, sweeping the landscape with darkening grey.

At last, realizing the futility of continuing the search in such conditions, Frank turned, and headed his mount towards a small kiddleywink huddled into a shadowed hollow. Like most inns of its type it was a dubious place with a bad reputation, but vagrants called there, tales were told, and news recounted from places further north. It was possible he might find some clue there pointing to Bethany's fate or Merynne's whereabouts.

He tethered his horse by an outhouse, in a sheltered place, and went in. The scene that met his eyes was unusual. A huddle of callers were gathered near the bar by a swinging oil lamp. From the muffled conversation between brief silences it was obvious that something was afoot. An accident, perhaps? Or had there been a fight, with murder done? Frank was prepared for anything as he pushed his way to the forefront of the furtive gang. His back stiffened at what he saw. At first he could hardly believe his own eyes. On a bench Merynne lay white-faced and still. Her eyes were open, and faint sounds came from her lips. Someone – a woman – probably the landlord's wife, was kneeling beside her, and had a flask in her hand. A trickle of the spirit coursed from Merynne's lips down her chin.

'You better now?' the woman was saying harshly, but not unkindly. 'You shouldn' a gone walkin' in your condition, an' with the rain comin. What's your name, eh? Wellan, edn et? From way back theer at Morningsgate?'

'That's right,' a man's voice was answered from nearby. 'I told you, when I brought 'er in. Merynne Drake as was.'

He glanced up and saw Frank towering above him. He was a bow-legged, whimsical looking customer with a shrewd look in his eyes. Tom Goyne. Seeing Frank, he gasped, 'Well, I'll be –'

Frank pushed him away and bent down, staring hard into Merynne's face. A combination of nerves, temper, and relief prompted him to take her by the shoulders and shake her back to life, scolding. But he restrained the impulse.

'Are you all right?' he asked, in a voice strangely gentle for him.

Merynne turned her face away. 'I just fell, that's all. Tom found me and brought me here. I was looking for Bethany.'

'You little –' Frank caught his lip and didn't finish. He eased his wife up a little, turned to the pedlar and said, 'I guess I should thank you, and I do.' He fumbled in his wallet and held out a coin towards the quaint bow-legged figure. Tom pushed his hand away. By then Merynne appeared to have drifted into a half sleep. 'I don't barter in human lives, surr. This lady's an old friend of mine. Known her since she was a li'l maid, I have. I don't want a payment for bringin' her to safety. Anyways –' his eyes twinkled, 'ole Gyppo seed her first. Stopped dead 'ee did givin' a neigh like ole Harry 'isself. An' there she was, lying all wisht an' white near one o' them murderous holes.' He stopped for a second, narrowing his eyes and said reprovingly, 'she shouldn' be left alone to go wanderin' – not in *her* state, surr.'

'What do you mean?'

The little man shrugged. 'Hasn' she said then? Well, you just pin her down an' ask, that's what I'd do. A woman wi' child in her belly gets funny ideas in her head sometimes; next time ole Gyppo mightn't be around to nose her out, poor young thing. An there's somethin' else – young Bethany –'

'*Yes?*' Frank's glance sharpened.

'I've got news. She's up country, Devon way with a tinker family, all dressed up as a little lad –'

'A *boy*?'

Goyne nodded. 'Bright lil' thing' too – for all her play actin' – managed to get me a message. They think her daft. But there's no daftness in *that* young body, surr –'

After the first shock of relief Frank's thought switched back to Merynne. 'I must get my wife home first, have they a cart here? A vehicle of any sort? She could ride with me, but –'

'Ole Gyppo's at the back. He's pulled more'n a lightweight than her in his time. If I walk we could manage, I reckon.'

'Right.'

In a few minutes Tom was leading his pedlar's cart up the short track to the moorland lane with Merynne inside padded by rugs, sacking and a pillow; Frank, at a leisurely canter and pausing at intervals, rode a little way ahead. The rain eased. Soon the dense darkness cleared to a watery light. The ground was sodden and progress was slow. But when they reached Morningsgate the movement and freshening damp air had revived Merynne sufficiently for her to be told simple facts.

'Bethany's whereabouts are roughly known,' Wellan told her. 'It's simply a matter now of locating the exact spot. I'm going out again to inform the authorities and maybe join in the search myself – you'll stay here, lie quietly in bed and behave. Mrs Duvonne will see to that, I'm sure.' Laurette, who was standing nearby, smiled and nodded.

Merynne made a gesture of protest.

'Why can't I –?'

'You know very well why not,' Frank interrupted. 'And when I get back, you young madam, you'll have some explaining to do. Still, that's for later.'

A little colour returned to Merynne's pale cheeks. 'Are you telling me the truth? Is Bethany *really* safe?'

'Why should I lie?' He swung round and strode to the door.

'Take care of her,' he said to Laurette, before leaving.

'Don't worry,' Laurette assured him. 'You can trust me.'

His answering glance held gratitude. Yes, he knew. She was the type of woman who could give everything, demanding nothing in return.

If only Merynne had something of the same capacity. But then, if she had, he would probably not desire her so passionately.

With which logical thought, he plunged out again into the wet night.

15

Knowing that Merynne would be completely attended by Laurette, Frank went out, and set off again on the first stage of a new search for Bethany. He had a wild hope that Rom and Thisbe might have an inkling of the tinkers' destination, although there was enmity between the two families, the former being of true Romany blood which gave them an aversion to mere travelling 'mumpers'. Still, most itinerants had haphazard contact from time to time, and there was no active bad feeling between himself and the gipsies except for Rom's mother who was so ancient she had nothing else to do but curse and utter ill omens.

Wellan knew of their new whereabouts, only two miles from Morningsgate, in a copse beneath a rocky, cavernous dip in the moors. The place was sheltered in bad weather, near a stream cutting down sharply towards the sea. It was on the border between common land and Morningsgate estate. Frank had not questioned their right to be there. One day, when the mood took them, they would be off again, meantime they gave no trouble. Rom even might prove useful, if an odd job man was ever needed.

So Frank rode purposefully through the fitful night with money in his wallet to bribe any information possible from the wanderers.

Horse and rider had only covered a short distance when the rain which had temporarily cleared, started again, lashing furiously from the west, increasing the sucking danger of the land's surface, swelling streams and pools to rivulets of mire. Once or twice the horse stumbled and he was nearly thrown. But at last he managed to locate the site of the gipsies. Wet and bedraggled, holding his mount by the bridle, he found them huddled in small vans under cover of a cave.

Rom, unheeding of the old woman's theatening raucous voice, grudgingly invited him to join Thisbe and himself, and when Wellan had explained, said broodingly, 'They're a greedy, thieving lot, them mumpers. If you want to catch 'em, master, you'll have to act, fast. Redlake's a way off, an' from theer they could've got to Devon by now.'

'I know that very well, man, but have you any idea of their route? North, west, or east? – you tell me and I've something for you here –' he opened his fist, showing a handful of coins, 'and this is yours.'

Rom, about to speak, was interrupted by the old woman. 'Don' you say nuthen,' she screeched. 'Them's dangerous folk,' she spat, 'An' we doan' want to go helpin' gorgios neither. Curse on 'em I say. Curse an' the devil tek 'em all.'

'Shut up,' Rom ordered, while Thisbe pushed the old creature back into the shadows. 'Yes,' he told Frank, 'maybe I c'n be a bit of use. Cut eastwards they do generally I've heard. Towards the bigger towns. There's a place called Brakeley – no more'n a big village. An inn theer – the Black Bull's run by a chap called Starke. Deals go on. Pilferin' of stolen goods an' such like. Wouldn' touch it myself – decent Romanies steer clear, but you mark my words it'll be a stoppin' place for such as them. An' that's all I *can* tell you.' He shrugged and turned away.

'Thanks,' Frank said. 'Tom Goyne thought they'd go east. Now you've endorsed it.'

'Ah. He'd be knowin',' Rom agreed. 'Haven't seen him lately. But then we haven' bin on the road much since Tallan and Sheba went.'

'I'm sorry about that.'

'As I said – it's the way of life. Animals, birds – an' the

small thin's crawlin', they have their day, short or long, an'
then its over. You can't shake the pattern o' Nature.'

Not wishing to waste any more time listening to Rom's
brooding philosophy, Frank paid what he'd promised and
started off again. His first impulse was to ride through the
night recklessly searching the north-east for the kidnappers.
But the weather and all other odds were against him. He'd
have to change horses en route and it was doubtful if he'd
strike the right track. By dawn, when he'd seen how his wife
was, at the house, he'd get messengers and the proper
authorities alerted. Tom Goyne had already promised to do
what he could, although it was unlikely he'd get anywhere
with that old donkey in such a furious storm, but would find
shelter again at the kiddleywink or some other available
place. So Wellan, half blinded by wind and rain, forced his
mount towards Morningsgate.

Suddenly his horse reared. A terrified whinny penetrated
the thunderous onslaught of tumbling earth and granite. A
boulder rushed by, crashing through gorse and undergrowth, missing them by only a yard or two. There was a
further flurry of stones driven on a rivulet of mud. Jagged
lightning lit the scene briefly, showing nothing but a great
slide of land roaring towards them. Frank kicked his mount
sharply, heading the frightened creature sharply to his right.
Sweat and rain streamed from their bodies. It was as though
hell itself was opening its gaping jaws to receive them, with
the legendary Tregeagle and his host of devils in pursuit.

On, and on, and on.

At last having miraculously evaded being taken by the
elements, horse and rider came to the bridge overlooking
Morningsgate.

Wellan reined abruplty. Horror filled him. Half the house
below was covered by a mound of earth. A wan light glowed
fitfully from a window at the side, then frailly flickered out.
He stared stupidly, aghast at the holocaust until a shower of
small stones hit his face, drawing blood. He came to life

again and bracing himself against the storm cut down to what had been their home.

Half of the building was mere rubble. In the eastern wing he found Laurette in a downstairs room, attending Merynne, who was propped up with cushions on a sofa. A servant girl was standing nearby, with a bowl and jug of water. In the grate a wan fire burned. Tiny Luke lay in a wooden cradle by the table.

'Whatever happened to her?' Frank shouted. 'Is she all right?'

Merynne opened her wide eyes, staring at him accusingly. She was very pale and white-lipped. Laurette also looked ill from strain.

'She will be, when she's recovered from the shock and a cut leg. She was on the stairs when it – when they collapsed. It was a bad fall. The girl and I managed to get her here. But of course –' her voice faltered. Frank knew what she meant.

'There'll be no baby now. Is that what you were going to say?' For some seconds Laurette didn't reply, then she answered, 'That's so. I'm sorry. But –' she got up and rested a hand on his shoulder, 'there can be others. Why not? The miracle is that she's alive at all.'

Very gently Wellan freed himself and looked down on Merynne.

'Everything's going to be fine,' he said. 'Don't worry – don't fret, love. I'm here. You've got me –'

'*You?*' Although her voice was weak, the contempt in it penetrated and stung him. He was about to protest, but was restrained by Laurette.

'Leave her now,' she said quietly. 'She doesn't know what she's saying –'

'She's said nothing,' he answered abruptly, and began again, 'Merynne, listen to me –'

'Oh go away. Don't you see I don't want you.'

With lowered head he turned and walked heavily to the door. Laurette followed.

'You must dry yourself. There are clothes in the kitchen. I saw they were ready –'

He threw her a brief grateful look.

'Thank you. Are the others all right? The boy and man?'

'All safe, sir. It's a mercy only one wing of the place was taken. I'm afraid there won't be much left. *What* a storm. And so sudden.'

'I'll have a look round.'

'Be careful. There's a lot of broken glass about. Wouldn't it be best to wait till the rain's eased?'

'Not much sign of that,' Frank replied curtly.

Although tired to the point of exhaustion, he felt the need of activity, anything to dispel the sight of Merynne's cold white face.

The rain continued until daylight, and presently, ironically, silvery sunlight climbed over a glassy still sea. All wind had gone, but devastation lay everywhere.

Most of all in Merynne's heart.

*

As soon as possible, Wellan made his way to Wheal Chace. He'd heard there'd been trouble and found it was true. New flaws in the old workings had given, due to the heavy rain, causing a collapse of the wall between an old shaft and one recently sunk nearby. Water from swollen moorland streams had merged into a river taking a diverted course to the mine; flooding had destroyed levels, and blocked adits. The result was disastrous. Although no lives were lost, which was miraculous, three miners were injured, one seriously.

'Failure,' Frank thought, staring round. 'Nothing but dam failure everywhere.' He realised glumly that this further collapse of his plans on top of The Ring venture would so heavily drain his pocket, his financial status could be in jeopardy. Experience across the Atlantic had proved how fortunes could be made and lost in a day. A rich man one moment could be a pauper the next. Not that he was in that category. He had assets still independent of copper or the Theatre, but the unforeseen present had landed him on the losing side, on top of which was the unsatisfactory relationship with his wife.

Sitting rigidly astride his horse, he surveyed the bleak scene with bitter distaste. He'd sell out, he'd have to. Wheal Chace and the tumbled walls of Morningsgate symbolised the end of an era, and with luck – the beginning of a new. His spirits rose a little. For once Fate had taken things out of his own hands. Except for Merynne he'd wipe all present concerns from his existence, salvaging what he could to commence on a fresh venture.

Where? How? What the hell did it matter at such a point? He'd never been a man to fret over pros and cons. Life was for living. And by God, he'd do it somehow, with Merynne by his side! Something would turn up – given the brains and guts to look for it.

He jerked his horse to movement, kicked it to a swift canter, and had taken the turn towards Morningsgate when a gang of men, miners, approached him from a side path. He'd have ridden on, but they blocked his way, forcing him to rein.

One anxious-eyed, with a belligerent thrust to his jaw, stepped forward. 'What do we do now, surr?' he asked. 'Where's the work for us in all this?'

Knowing desperate men could be dangerous, Wellan answered ambiguously, 'Take a look. There's plenty for any willing to tackle it.'

'And payment? Wages? Will they go on?'

Poor devils, Frank thought with a pang of sympathy; they were already envisaging hungry bellies to feed with nothing coming in. He'd have to contact the shareholders and adventurers to see if any financial help would be forthcoming from some joint effort. He himself would hardly be in a position to do much.

He forced himself to say, 'Have I ever let you down? Haven't I provided work for you when I could have kept my

hands in my pocket for my own benefit? What makes you
doubt me now?'

'The land – we're miners. We know the earth. What we
doan' know is y'r own pocket. How're y' goin' t' get copper
out o' this muck? An' if you doan'? What then? Where's our
livelihood comin' from?'

'I'm not God,' Frank answered with a spurt of temper.
'You'd better go to your chapels and pray. Maybe you'll get
an answer and be luckier than me.'

He loosened his rein and rode through the group,
justifying his words and action by the knowledge that the
sooner the men guessed the truth the better. There was
really no point in prevarication.

Back at Morningsgate he did his best to make peace with
Merynne. With her support he was convinced he could still
provide a rewarding future. But she turned away from him.

'It's because of the baby,' Laurette assured him. 'She'll
recover. It will take time. And when Bethany's found –' her
voice trailed off.

Bethany! Of course. His mind was suddenly jerked to this
other so important problem, and the rest of that day, apart
from the troublesome work of dealing with the mining
business, was given to setting further enquiries afoot
concerning his missing daughter.

16

By every means possible search for the missing 'boy' was speedily got under away. But slowness of transport, the numerous twisting byways used by itinerants and cunning closeness of 'travellers' when legal authority became involved, made progress difficult. Landlords of kiddley-winks and inns were also chary of supplying any useful information that might lead to trouble on their part. Mouths for the most part were sealed. If anyone had seen a tow-haired boy passing through a certain locality, no one said. The tinkers themselves got to know of the increased hue-and-cry, and kept the child hidden.

'You can't do et forever,' old Jetta told Cora, the woman, forebodingly. 'Best get rid of 'er soon as possible. Chuck 'er out at some lonely spot where no one'll look – give 'er naught to eat an' let 'er fend f'r 'erself. She'll soon be a gonner. There's nuthen any more but trouble for us while we kip 'er eer.'

'You're a fine one to talk,' Cora snapped. 'The whole cause of the thing you are. If you hadn't picked 'er up in the first place there'd be no worry now.'

A gnarled, evil smile revealing a yellow fang of tooth twisted the old woman's lips. 'An' poorer in the pocket you'd be,' she said, slyly. 'A small fortune she's bin, an' doan you forget it.'

'*Fortune*? What use is that? If we land up getting shipped to one o' them furrin places or worse.'

'Get rid of 'er,' the old woman reiterated. 'It's the only way.'

And on a dark night of rain and high winds they did.

The spot chosen for Bethany's abandonment was eight miles from any village, in a lane seldom used even by a farm labourer. The ground was soggy with mud and water driven down to the valley from surrounding hills. No sign of a building was in sight – not even a barn. The sky was moonless, without a single star penetrating the heavy cloud.

Bethany shivered and tried to draw back when the man opened the door of the van, one hand ruthlessly clenched round her shoulder.

'It's raining –' she cried. 'Don't, please, don't –'

He gave her a relentless shove. The woman, in a sudden fit of pity and fear, threw a hunk of bread after her. 'There y'are. Eat it – you'll be all right –' she shouted. The man pulled her back and slammed the door, after which he struck her hard across the face.

The old woman laughed. There was the crack of a whip, and the cart moved ahead, leaving the solitary small figure of a little girl wearing a boy's ragged clothes, standing under the dripping trees.

For some time she walked and scrambled, tears from her eyes mingling with the downpour of the rain. At last, exhausted, she fell into a ditch. Cold leaves and dripping grass slapped her face. Once some small wild creature of the night muzzled and sniffed her cheek, but she did not know. Sleep and the chill of weariness had already claimed her. At first she'd had a confused dream of Torgale weaving some magic spell that took her back to the farm and a kind man called Will. Then Will turned into a wonderful giant who picked her up in strong arms and called her 'princess'. After that everything became dark and frightening – a confusion of wild sounds and ugly shapes. She screamed once, then all was quiet.

Some time later, quite by chance a Methodist Pastor, Samuel Hawken, riding home from a meeting of an outlying hamlet found her.

Astonished and shocked, he reined, and leading his mount by the bridle, went to investigate.

He thought at first she was dead. But when he touched her, she stirred.

'Thank God,' he said aloud.

He lifted her up, took off his own coat, wrapped her in it, and placed her on his horse before him. Half an hour later they reached his own home by a wayside chapel, strangely enough called Bethel.

The granite abode was small, simple, and sparsely furnished. But his good wife had a hot meal of broth and potatoes waiting.

'My dear soul!' she cried, 'what's this?'

She gave a close look at the small wet figure as her husband laid her on a narrow sofa.

He explained, and she shook her head sadly. 'I do believe this isn't a boy at all, Samuel,' she remarked.

The little girl opened her eyes then.

'I'm Bethany,' she said in a weak voice. 'And my papa's – my pa's –' she couldn't finish.

'That's all right, dear,' the Minister's wife said soothingly, 'you must have something warm to drink, and have those wet clothes taken off, then a nice long sleep. In the morning you can tell us all about it.'

So it was, that Bethany, following a long tortuous adventure came at last to safety, while her mother, at Morningsgate, steeled herself to feel nothing for any human being again, – neither husband, child, or friend, not even the tiny Luke.

*

Bethany slept that night by the stove of the kitchen in the Minister's house. The dwelling was cramped and their life frugal; he and his wife were people dedicated to their religion. He was a pioneer of his kind who had done mission work in remote parts overseas, including the mountains of Spain. His marriage had been one of purpose rather than romance. Ann Hawken, his wife, was a plain, physically strong woman capable of facing any emergency stoically. Her philosophy was simple. Whatever strange event came their way was the plan of God, and Bethany's entrance into their existence was, she averred, no exception.

'It must have been meant, Samuel,' she told her husband. 'The poor child has been neglected and abandoned most cruelly, and the good Lord has directed her into our care.'

Samuel Hawken, who had heard nothing of the little girl's disappearance – his duties only took him to the wildest and most remote places – nodded. 'You may be right, my dear. She shall stay with us while God wills it.'

'Forever perhaps,' Ann said. 'From the sound and look of her she's been in heathen company far too long. Our duty is to teach her the truth, Samuel, so she may learn to be a Christian.'

Samuel eyed his wife discerningly. 'Go cautiously, my dear,' he said. 'We know nothing of her background. Young things need care and understanding. And don't grow *too* fond of her. Her own people may turn up.'

Ann sniffed. 'I sincerely hope not. They must be wicked-minded creatures to allow any child so young to get into such a state.'

It was eleven o'clock the next morning when Bethany woke. Ann had shortened a cotton shift and other simple clothing for her, and after the little girl had been washed and dressed she had a cup of milk to drink and a bowl of porridge. Then Ann started questioning.

At first, Bethany did not reply. Wonderment, fear, awe and longing for Frank, churned through her brain in a whirl of emotions. But when at last she found her tongue it was difficult to stop her flow of chatter. She recounted her wild unpleasant experience of being kidnapped by the tinkers, and how lovely it had been before that, when her papa had let her perform at the theatre.

'There was Vonny, too,' she said. 'Vonny was nice, and everyone clapped when I danced. Mr Gaylord wanted me to go with them, but papa said I was too little yet –'

Ann Hawken gasped with horror.

'You *danced*? At one of those wicked places? A *theatre*?'

'Oh it wasn't wicked. It was *nice*,' Bethany said, smiling. There was a pause before she added, 'There was Torgale too.'

'Torgale?'

'He was a – a kind of magic thing,' Bethany said, more seriously, sensing that it would be very difficult properly to explain Torgale to this kind but rather severe-looking lady.

'What do you mean by magic, child?' Ann enquired.

Bethany shook her head.

'He was only a stone, really, a big stone where I lived with my mother before she took me to papa. I had two papas you know –'

Ann shook her head dumbly. The more the little girl told her, the more confused her background seemed to become!

'Well,' she forced herself to say presently, 'we must forget all those things now –'

'But I don't *want* to forget,' Bethany protested. 'I *want* to dance and be with papa – my *real* papa. And I want to see Vonny again. And Torgale –'

'We can't always do just what we want my dear,' Ann said primly. 'There are so many good things to learn about –'

'Good things aren't always nice –'

'And nice things are sometimes very wicked.'

'Are they? Why?'

Ann sighed.

'Whilst you're here child, you mustn't ask so many questions. I have a large book – it's called The Bible. Have you ever heard of it?'

'You mean the one about praying and things, and Jesus?'

'Yes, yes. It's a *true* book, and the stories are real. This afternoon we will sit down together and I'll read one to you.'

'If you like,' Bethany agreed grudgingly, 'then I'll tell you about Torgale.'

As matters turned out, the opportunity did not arise.

Two hours later Pastor Hawken, who'd taken a short morning service at a remote hamlet five miles away, returned and informed his wife of the child's identity.

'There was a notice nailed to the chapel wall,' he said, 'and it obviously refers to her. I must be off again to inform the authorities.'

'Oh *no*, Samuel. If you'd heard the things she's been telling me –'

'It's my duty – *our* duty my dear,' the pastor said firmly. 'She was sent to us by God for refreshment and succour. But her life lies elsewhere.'

'Very well. Yes. You're quite right of course. But – I shall pray for her.'

'We will both pray for her, my dear,' he said. 'And now, let me tell her she'll soon be with her father again, and try and join in her happiness. To be glum isn't what we're born for, but to give joy, and laugh sometimes.'

That evening, Bethany was fetched by Frank and taken in the family chaise to a luxurious coaching house only two miles from the devastated Morningsgate, where the family were ensconsed in private quarters until their home had been put into sufficient order for their return.

Merynne, pale and outwardly composed, felt a rush of tears flood her eyes when she pulled the little girl to her. But Bethany drew herself away.

'I'm all right,' she said. 'I've had an adventure.'

'*All right?* But it's been *terrible* for us not knowing what had happened. Don't you *understand?* Don't you?'

Bethany ran to her father and placed her face against his coat. Sensing her inward distress, he patted the ragged hair soothingly. 'Be nice to your mama, princess,' he said. 'She's been poorly.'

Bethany turned slowly, and stared at Merynne with

solemn, searching eyes. '*Have* you, Mama? What sort of poorliness? Like Luke?'

'Luke isn't poorly,' Merynne said in a tired voice. 'He's just – not as strong as you are. That's why I – why we have to take such care of him.'

'Will he ever grow up and be big like me? I was a boy you know. They made me into one. That's why they cut my hair,' she lifted her chin proudly. 'I wasn't frightened, not a bit, not really. Sometimes it was fun being able to pick flowers without any shoes on, and walk in the streams. People liked me too. They gave me things. We used to knock at doors, and sometimes I had sweets –' She broke off as Merynne put a shred of handkerchief to her lips and hurried to the door.

Wellan gave his daughter a hug and went after her. 'Wait there,' he told Bethany. 'I'll send Vonny to you.'

There was a snap of the latch. A minute later Laurette's quick footsteps could be heard hurrying up the hall.

Frank reached Merynne at the top of the stairs and with his arm round her waist led her to her room.

Once inside she pushed him away. 'Don't worry,' she said stiffly, 'I'd rather not be fussed over. Bethany needs you.'

His mouth tightened. 'And you do not?'

She shrugged, and went to the window. 'I'm really very tired. It's all been such a strain, and now she's back, I – I really *would* like to try and relax without any more emotional scenes. You've got your daughter again –'

'Our daughter,' he corrected her.

Merynne turned her head and looked him straight in the eyes, with a cold cynical little smile on her lips.

'Oh I don't think you need include me,' she answered. 'I bore her, that's all. There'll not be another, and perhaps it's as well.'

He was beside her again in a second, hands gripping her shoulders.

'Don't talk to me in that way,' he told her, with his face close to hers. 'You know very well no one can say.'

'The specialist did, didn't he? The one the doctor brought?'

'Not definitely,' Frank replied firmly, trying to sound convincing. 'Remember doctors don't know everything. He said so himself. The important thing is to regain your physical and mental strength.'

She sighed. 'I'm not deranged. He was very – explicit. Oh Frank, don't try to – don't *lie*. I can't have any more children. That's the truth. And now please do leave me. I'm sorry to be so morbid. I shall get over all this, in time.'

'Of course you will,' he spoke cheerfully. 'And we're lucky I'd say – two kids to bring up, and one that's going to take a hell of a lot of energy to control.'

She said nothing to his remark. Feeling awkward, he kissed her lightly on the cheek. He had no way of assessing her feelings – women were strange creatures, but the interview with the two medical men following her miscarriage must have been very difficult for her. He had been shocked himself, and more than a little disappointed at the verdict. Certain injuries of course, on top of strain, shock, and female complications he didn't understand, meant simply that any further pregnancy would not only be dangerous but impossible.

'Otherwise,' the specialist had said, with a smile meant to put everything right, 'Mrs Wellan will be a perfectly fit woman, and your married life together will have no impediment. You already have two children, so your future should be an exceedingly happy one.'

But would it be?

As Frank went downstairs he reflected glumly on Merynne's fatalistic mood. Somehow, he decided, she and Bethany must be brought closer. There was Luke, too. Even her first passion for Will's boy seemed now to be fading. Poor little devil. A stab of sympathy for the youngster seized him suddenly. He'd take him in hand, show more interest, and see that his daughter did the same. If this could be achieved the family might draw closer together. Bethany would always be nearest his heart, because she was his own. But obviously she needed more control. He wanted her as she was – passionate, expressive, free and natural as the wild creatures of the moors – as the winds and rains sweeping the sun-splashed hills, and the great waves pounding the cliffs. One day, though, she would become a young woman destined for other things. He must see she was fitted to fill the role of a lady, and bear children with an honoured place in society.

His daughter.

Pride filled him. He would dearly have liked a son as well.

This apparently was not to be, so he had to accept it, Merynne too.

Merynne.

For the first time he sensed her suffering and knew in that moment there could never be another woman in his life.

Somehow he had to win her all over again.

17

During the next weeks Merynne appeared mostly indifferent when Frank made overtures to heal their relationship. Any attempt at love-making became farcical. Her aloof, apparent coldness chilled him. He could not understand – neither did she completely understand herself – although beneath the reserved facade she secretly longed for warmth and affection. If only she could dispel the shadow of Will's death! – if only she hadn't lost the baby! – if only Bethany didn't so openly resist her, or Frank would pay less attention to the little girl! As things were Merynne felt unwanted – a mere incident in his existence. Meanwhile Wellan was looking for another house. The foundations of Morningsgate had suffered more drastically than was at first believed. To have the place in proper condition again would cost a little fortune, and he no longer had that to spare. Except for a minor shareholding he had pulled out of Wheal Chace. A certain interest in The Ring remained, and he had collateral at the bank – none of which, at the moment, brought in sufficient income to keep the family living indefinitely at the Coach-house.

Merynne had little to do while Laurette was with them, which increased her lackadaisical attitude. When Mrs Duvonne had gone, joining Gaylord Werne and Toby Finch for a tour of the West Country and Midlands, things improved a little. Luke was still a rather delicate boy needing more attention than most children of his age, and something of the old bond was revived between the mother and son. But Bethany with her natural perspicacity realised it, and became even more attached to her father.

Once, after a sharp scene with Merynne, she ran to Frank and said a trifle petulantly, 'I don't like it here, Papa. Can't we go somewhere else?

'Why? What's the matter? What's wrong, Princess?'

'Well –' she considered for a moment, then continued, 'there's nothing to do. Mama's always cuddling Luke, or cross. And there's no magic anywhere.'

The large eyes raised to his were so brilliant, so pleading and full of an emotion he couldn't understand, he drew her childish body closer and asked, 'What do you mean by "magic"? The theatre?'

She nodded. 'Partly. But there's Torgale too.'

'You mean that old stone – near the farm.'

'Yes. I could be anyone when I was with Torgale. Even when it rained I liked it there. The grass made singing sounds when the wind blew. And do you know, Papa, there was something else –'

'What was that, love?'

'Those little jumping things –'

He laughed.

'Now don't tell me you've been mixing with spriggans?'

She shook her head.

'Of course not. There aren't any, are there? But the grasshoppers were real. I know they were grasshoppers, Anne told me, and they swung on grasses when it was summer and trilled and trilled. It was funny. Of course, they weren't singing, not like the grass. It was just that they were rubbing their legs together.'

'You seem to know quite a bit about nature,' Frank remarked.

'You mean the trees and rabbits and foxes, and the path down to Cragga? Oh yes. When Tallan and Sheba were there they told me lots and lots of funny secret things.' The childish voice died into sadness.

Wellan lifted her up suddenly and when her face was level with his, said, 'Cragga isn't a good place for children to go to, Princess. But maybe – if you promise to behave and do what I tell you – we'll go back one day to the farm. Would you like that?'

Her solemn face broke into a radiant smile.

'To *live*, do you mean? Oh yes, Papa, if you were there, and I *would* promise, I would really, I'd never *never* go to Cragga alone.'

He put her down.

'We shall have to see then.'

The conversation ended there; but the next day Frank, on a visit to the mine, made an extra journey to Tarnefell.

It was late afternoon when he arrived there.

The fading sunlight cut slantwise across the front of the building, accentuating the elongated shadow of weeds and overgrown bushes, of empty windows staring bleakly across the wild landscape. Occasionally the fitful light gave a curious impression of watchful life. No one had lived there after Merynne left. The place was considered a 'white elephant' since Drake's death. But suddenly it presented, to Frank, a challenge. The old sense of adventure stirred in him.

'I could make something of it,' he thought. 'The building's still good. I could bargain with the owner and get it for a song, probably. Never tried farming in my life. But Merynne knows it. Being a lady doesn't suit her all that well – a bit of hard work might bring her back to her senses, and being a proper wife.'

The more he considered the idea, the more plausible it became. The building could be extended, the surrounding land seawards – or at least part of it – brought under control for the production of crops. The moors behind weren't sufficiently verdant for dairy farming, but sheep would do well, for the short-legged Cornish breed. The thought of being involved in manual work once more appealed to him.

He'd been sitting on his backside lately more than was natural for a man of his type. By God! Maybe there was a pattern to life after all, and things would work out for the best.

Jack-of-all-trades – gold digger, man of property and mines – gentleman farmer! and from there? – who could say! He and Merynne might yet become Lord and Lady of a vast estate. Nothing worth aiming for was beyond achieving, given the guts and will to do it.

He rode back to the coaching house in a lively mood.

Merynne was upstairs in their private apartment trying to amuse Bethany before she had her supper and went to bed. He thought how beautiful she looked, in a simply cut blue gown of some soft material draped lower than usual on the shoulders, and caught by a single white flower at the hollow just above the shadowed valley of her breasts. The shining waves of hair were drawn to the back of her head in a mass of curls. He had a passionate urge at that moment to possess her.

He went forward, touched a shoulder gently, and said, 'Merynne, love –'

She stared at him, as a rush of wild-rose colour flooded her cheeks.

'Yes?'

'I want to talk to you. I want –'

'Bethany's just going to have her supper.'

'Bethany can wait.'

'Oh but –'

'The girl can attend to that. Or Mrs Pendrake. You know she's more than willing to take charge.'

'Yes, but it will soon be opening time.'

'Never mind, for once put me and our personal affairs first.'

In the end Merynne agreed. Bethany was ushered into the care of the innkeeper's wife, leaving Frank and his wife together. He led her into the bedroom which was already prepared for the night. The silk quilt on the four-poster canopied bed had already been turned back; candles were flickering on the dressing table and Merynne's lacy night clothes were laid out on a chair. A log fire glowed from the grate. Inwardly apprehensive, Merynne went to the window, pulled the curtains a little aside, and pretended to be interested in the moonlit sky. Silvered clouds passed intermittently driven on a thin breeze from the sea, sending long shadows streaking down the moor.

She waited, with one hand over her heart, and said in low tones, 'What is it Frank? What do you want? What have we to talk about?'

Treading softly, he came up behind her, pulled her round and drew her to him. His lips were warm and demanding on hers. She made an effort to resist him, then suddenly gave in. For a few heady seconds they stood bemused, as one, while resentment died into mutual response. Then, shaking a little, she pulled herself away.

He laughed quietly.

'You see, love? You don't hate me so much after all.'

Confused, she pushed by him, crossed to the mirror, and made a pretence of tidying her hair.

'I never did hate you, Frank. It's just that we see things so differently. There's nothing in our lives to agree on –'

'No? Well, when I've told you what I have in mind maybe you'll change your opinion.'

She turned. His serious expression brought a puzzled frown to her face.

'What is it?' she asked.

'Sit down and relax.'

She did so automatically. He stood, with his arms behind his back, watching her, ready for any slight change of expression of varying mood as he unfolded his new idea.

'I've a mind to buy Tarnefell,' he said abruptly.

She was astounded.

'*Tarnefell*? Whatever for? *Why*? – you're joking.'

He shook his head.

'Not me. Not this time. It's going to waste as it is. And you lived there – you liked it –'

'With Will,' she interrupted.

'Yes. That's just it.'

'What do you mean?'

'I think you know, Merynne, or could make a good guess. All this time you've held a grudge – thought I'd had a hand in what happened. He's stood between us like a ghost. Well, I'm going to lay it for good. Isn't that what they call it? Think I'd return to a place with my family expecting to see a spectre lurking round every corner? There'll be no ghost there when I've done what I intend to with it – nor in your heart either –' he paused, adding after a moment, '– but there hasn't been, has there? – not deep down. You never wanted him in the way *we* feel? Never did, never could. It's been guilt with you all along.'

'No. Why should *I* feel guilty? What for? It was *you* who – who –'

'I know. You needn't say it. I was with him, we had a shindy, and he went off his head. That's the truth of it. All the same it was a damn good thing he *did* kick the bucket. A man who goes and shoots himself over any other man or woman alive isn't the best person to have charge of a wild rebellious creature like you, or of a young son. You just see things straight for once, my love. This life's for living, and getting the best out of things – not to moon and fret over dead bones. I suppose in a way he wasn't a bad chap. He worked hard, but my God, Merynne, Tarnefell can be made to thrive and be a landmark for sore eyes – a home fit for you and Bethany, and –'

He kept back the words in time. But it was too late. She knew.

'You were going to say for all the other children we'll have, weren't you?'

He bent down, gripped her shoulders, and pulled her to her feet.

'Maybe, I'd have liked more, but it's not important, so long as I have you. Understand?' He shook her. 'Get that into your head once and for all, will you, and listen to me –'

She protested, but only for a moment. When he'd released her, she sighed, went back to the bed, and waited.

Gradually, something of his enthusiasm penetrated her inertia. This was not the wealthy self-made Frank Wellan talking, but Nat Herne, the young adventurer she'd first married – domineering, eager, wilful, filled with the fiery zest for living that had driven him overseas to make a fortune. For *her*, he'd said, and perhaps after all, it was true. But as a farmer? Would he be content? Only if he could make the success of it on a large scale. That was Nat's trouble – or perhaps 'excitement' of him, was the better way of putting it – everything he tackled or aimed for – his very physical self – had to be larger than life.

When he'd finished talking she was smiling a little.

He saw it, knelt down, and pulled her into his arms.

'How I love you,' he said, with her head pressed against his chest, '– and it's only the beginning –'

Yes, she thought, it was always that way with Nat. Nat – the old name came from her lips naturally, 'Oh Nat, Nat.'

Later he corrected her with a whimsical smile. '*Frank*; we're in for another new start, love,' he said. 'Wellan, remember? Frank Wellan and his lady, Mrs Merynne Wellan –'

'Of course.'

It didn't matter; names weren't important. What mattered was that they were beginning all over again. She had no way of knowing or even remotely guessing what the new phase was to entail.

If she had, her reactions to moving to Tarnefell would have been very different.

18

Once Frank's decision had been finally accepted by Merynne, he set to work with zest consulting architects and builders for extension to the farm and enclosure of land that had been left wild before. He found an agent willing to shoulder responsibility as farm manager, at the same time safeguarding his right to have the last word on any controversial point. Because of the expense – he'd had to pay more than he'd expected for the property – he took simpler accommodation at the inn on reduced financial terms. Merynne although elated by his intermittent love-making, was by then mostly bewildered; the prospect of returning to Tarnefell pleased her in many ways, but at times her husband's reckless enthusiasm frightened her. Looking ahead she knew there would be moments of memory that couldn't be entirely erased; finance, too, bothered her. Wellan had now sold all his shareholding in Wheal Chace and the other mine. When she made the effort to reason with him, suggesting he didn't after all know much about farming, and that it would take years probably to see any reasonable profit, he dismissed the fact lightly, grinned disarmingly, and stifled her words with a kiss.

'I've never failed yet,' he told her. 'When I tackle anything it's to succeed. You should know that by now, love.'

Yes, she well knew the wild, ambitious side of him, and tried to accept in this case that he was right. But suppose he wasn't? Suppose he had to face defeat? Generally she managed to put the niggling possibility aside. The period was too exciting for depression. Bethany also was wildly thrilled.

'I'll see Torgale again,' she said, 'and the badgers, and all the little jumping things. And Tom Goyne and Gyppo. Will Rom and Thisbe be there?'

'Perhaps, perhaps not,' Frank told her in a more serious voice than usual. 'In any case, love, you'll have to remember you're a princess now. *My* princess, and not go wandering about all day talking to tinkers and tramps.'

'Rom isn't a tramp,' Bethany protested quickly. 'His grandpa was an Egyptian King –'

'And who told you that?'

'Thisbe. Where's Egypt, Papa?'

'Oh a long way from here. Too far for us ever to go there, and you mustn't believe everything Rom or Thisbe told you. Rom's grandpa was a very old man and old people sometimes make up stories when they've nothing better to do.'

'Like me, you mean?'

'No,' Wellan gave her a light slap and a hug, 'not like you at all. You're a rascal. We're a couple of rascals, you and I.'

Bethany giggled, thinking how lovely it was that her wonderful father always seemed to have the right answer to her questions.

Months passed; months in which Frank dedicated himself fanatically to the Tarnefell project. It was spring when they moved in; patches of tender green feathered the trees and moors, the air was fresh, laden with the sweetness of bursting, growing things. A cook and a boy had been installed in the house, and two men, one an experienced hedgecutter, the other a labourer, came from their homes daily. An ex-miner, John Pengelly, was given employment to assist in any way possible, and Ned Pierce, an old shepherd, who was weary of having nothing to do, was once more reinstated to mind the sheep.

Frank did not have to be told he could no longer afford such current outlay with nothing coming in. But he wasn't bothered. He'd faced far worse circumstances before, and managed not only to come through, but make a fortune from enterprise. He could do it again. A man incapable of taking risks wasn't worth his salt, and this time Merynne was the prize – not the Merynne who was pliant and rewarding in his arms again, but the Merynne who could give herself utterly, with her mind as well as her body, trusting him and believing in him completely.

'I thought you said we had to economise,' she remarked one day, 'and that there'd be a lot for me to do when the farm got going. Instead we've got a girl and a cook, and men coming in and out – why? Don't you think I'm capable of lifting a hand any more?'

'You've the children to look after,' he pointed out, 'and the household management – the dairy – I've decided to have a few cattle after all, and I reckon it might interest you how to pull an udder –'

'Pull an udder? Oh, Frank, what a way of putting it, and anyway, you've always said cattle weren't practical for Tarnefell.'

'I've changed my mind.' He spoke abruptly. 'There's nothing beyond us now. *Nothing.*'

She sighed. 'Oh, I don't know. If only we could be a bit – a bit *settled* for a time. Everything's changing so quickly. We never seem to have time to sit back, or wander –' Her voice trailed off.

'What do you mean by that? Travel?'

She shook her head, staring at him with eyes holding the luminosity of moorland pools. 'No, not travel, just *live.*'

His arm slipped round her waist, drawing her close.

'I reckon we do plenty of that, love.'

She pulled herself away.

'There are other things than lying in bed, and – and –'

'Fornicating?' He laughed.

That stung her.

'I wouldn't call it that. You can be crude sometimes.'

He shrugged. 'My way of talk. *Man*'s talk.'

'I happen to be a woman.'

In two strides he'd reached and pulled her into his arms again. 'Of course you are – the sweetest, wildest, most tantalising creature in the world, and one day, my love, we're going to stand on the ridge together by that old stone circle near Bethany's Torgale, and see a whole new estate sprung from old roots –' His gaze glowed, bright with a fanatical fire, envisaging his own kingdom of the future with new hamlets and villages spreading south, east, and west – a kingdom ruled over by Merynne and himself, as chieftains ruled in the far-off past.

He didn't hear Merynne's sigh before she said, 'You're so excessive, Nat.'

'Nat?'

She nodded.

'You always will be. There's no escape, ever, from being what you really are.'

Those few words were to prove more prophetic than either of them dreamed of, at the time.

*

Because of the constant change and excitement of the effort to get life at Tarnefell into a workable routine, time passed quickly.

One evening in April of the following year Merynne saw a familiar shape moving slowly towards the farm along the lower moor lane. The animal, a donkey, plodded wearily with head thrust forward, as though pulling an almost unbearable load. As the vehicle drew nearer, the driver's hat, with a feather in it, was clearly discernible through a brief flash of dying sunlight. Old Tom Goyne and Gyppo.

Merynne, who'd been busy in the kitchen, sped down the hall to the door which was half open, and pushed it wider.

As the wheels of the cart grated and stopped, she ran to the gate and saw that the pedlar had something in a large basket by his side. The usual collection of nick-nacks and mixed assortment of fancy wares were stacked behind in their normal fashion, but the basket obviously contained something very special.

She waited until Tom descended and came towards her. He smiled, but the impish quality was no longer on his face.

'I should've been here before, my maid,' he said, drawing a hand across his brow, 'but old Gyppo's feelin' the weight o' his years more'n more as the days pass. An' this – that theer –' he cocked a thumb towards the cart – 'is heavier than you'd think. Extra weight counts when you've reached our age. Still, a promise is a promise, an' I did tell 'er – that furrin woman you had – I'd see 'ee was all right.'

'What foreign woman? Who? I don't understand,' Merynne said, 'who are you talking about?'

Tom studied her for a moment or two, shaking his head slowly, then he said, 'The lady – Mrs Duvonne. Laurette she called herself – she's sent you something. There's a letter with it. But –'

'A letter? Oh, Tom, do explain. And what's the – what has she sent?'

'A baby, ma'am.' The words came out abruptly. 'She could only think of you and Mr – Wellan. The company's doing badly, and Toby and Mr Gaylord thought you were the rightful folk to have the chile.'

'But why a baby? And if Laurette wanted to see me why couldn't she come herself?'

'Because she's dead, m'dear. Died 'avin' 'im.'

Still in a daze Merynne ran to the cart and peered into the basket. A tiny round face with a reddened button nose and brown eyes peering beneath a thatch of dark reddish hair, stared up at her.

'But –' A shock of awareness, a certain likeness in the tiny face to Frank, suddenly took the colour from her lips and cheeks, and for a moment the pedlar thought she was going to faint.

'He's a nice little thing,' he said half-apologetically, 'bin no trouble on the way. I was given a bottle o' course, but to tell you the truth I'll be glad to be rid of it – the responsibility I mean.'

There was a pause before Merynne asked, 'Whose child is it? Laurette wasn't married, was she?'

Old Tom looked away. 'No, no, ma'am. Nuthen like that.'

'You mean –?' Merynne's voice died before the question could be formed.

'She'd great faith in you, you an' Mr Wellan,' Tom resumed sadly. ' "Tell them to care for the li'l thing," she said, "but they will, they surely will. Merynne was good to me," she said, "an' Mr Wellan will understand." I don't rightly know the truth o' things myself, but seems to me not hard to guess.'

'No.' The word was a tight little sound on Merynne's lips.

Tom gave her a pleading look. 'She said something else too, m'dear, before she died. She said, "Ask her to forgive me. I didn't want to hurt no one. An' tell her she was the only one Frank ever loved. It was my fault," she said – "all my doin' because of tryin' to comfort him. But I meant nuthen to him." '

'I see.'

'Do you? I hope so.' The old man gave a sigh that ended in a rattling cough.

'You'd better have something to eat, and drink,' she said lifelessly, 'before you leave. Come with me.'

'And him? The li'l one?'

Merynne eyed the baby distastefully. She was on the brink of saying, 'Take it back with you. It's nothing to do with me,' but changed her mind when she saw Frank approaching from a nearby field.

'Oh well – yes, of course. We've plenty of milk. But I'll have to talk things over with – with Frank. I'm not sure yet what to think. You arrive with a child you say is Laurette's, and suggest –'

Old Tom reached out and patted one of her hands gently before fetching the baby. 'These things happen in life,' he said. 'Whether for good or ill that depends mostly on how you take them, m'dear. Doan' try probin' an' guessin' too much. There's many an unwanted weed sprung up to give a rich blossoming. One day, maybe old nature'll bring you happiness when you doan expect it.'

He walked away and returned in a few minutes carrying the bundle.

The child had only just been placed on a settee in the front parlour when Frank arrived. The pedlar muttered a few words in his ear and before Wellan could get over the shock, had turned and hurried back to his cart where Gyppo was patiently waiting.

Frank and Merynne stared at each other. During the brief silence he took a quick glance at the child, then looked again at his wife.

'Is it true?' she asked. '*Can* it be?'

'Tom doesn't lie,' he said bluntly. 'And I'm not going to. It *could* be. But if you just relax and listen to me for a bit possibly you'll understand –'

'*Understand?*' The word, the calm assumption that she could so calmly accept the situation, infuriated and distressed her so deeply she had to grip the back of a chair to prevent herself from falling. 'You had an affair with that woman behind my back, pretending to me she was just a house-keeper, a servant – when all the time you were lusting and lying with her in secret –' Her heart quickened painfully. 'How *could* you? – I never liked her. There was always something treacherous and foreign about her. She managed to turn Bethany against me, and then ensnared you. Or didn't you need ensnaring, Frank? Had you connived it all? Wasn't I enough? With Will out of the way didn't I have enough appeal to satisfy you? It was always the same with you, wasn't it? – a challenge! the fight to be one up on someone else?'

'Stop it,' he cried, with his voice rising to check the violent flow of words. 'It wasn't like that at all. Laurette Duvonne just happened to have a grain of sympathy and warmth in her – the sympathy you've never had – at a time when you were cold to me, making me feel the lowest scum on earth –'

'I –'

'Listen to me,' he shouted, 'and look back. Remember the time before Bethany was found? The way you spat and scratched at me like some wild cat when all I wanted was to have you as any man has his wife when there's trouble? For weeks you'd kept yourself off – shut the door on me as though I was scum. But that night I told myself it'd be different – we were both suffering together. Together maybe we could find a bit of comfort. Oh I wanted you then, Merynne – wanted you above all things – as a woman. Mistress, wife, mother and comforter – the whole damn lot. But *you* – all you could do with your icy, uppity airs, was to humiliate and deny me. Petty revenge was it? Because of Will –?' He paused a moment, and when she didn't answer, continued, 'So I took the only way out I know – drank myself sick and it was then Laurette found me. Somehow she quietened me and gave the release I wanted. That was it – *release*! from your coldness and contempt. Oh I know very well you despise me. Why you should – God knows. But I tell you one thing –' his expression became hard and relentless, 'at the moment I despise you too. Because you can tirade and shriek at me, when Laurette's dead, and her child lies there – needing a woman's care –'

'I don't want her child here, or anything that was hers.'

Even in her own ears Merynne's voice sounded like a stranger's, hard, without pity or gentleness.

'Whether you want it or not, this baby will remain. He happens to be my responsiblity, my son. If you can't accept him, I'll find another who can – some motherly woman grateful to have a home, a good job, and a child in her care, and you can devote yourself entirely to Luke.'

'Also Bethany.'

'No. Not Bethany. Unless I'm very much mistaken you're already somewhat low in Bethany's esteem, and I'll see in future she has no chance to soften the relationship.'

He turned, picked up the baby from the couch and strode into the hall. Merynne stood speechless by the table until she heard him calling to the daily girl. This was followed by the sound of conversation and footsteps going up the stairs. Then there was the slam of a door.

As though she was in some terrible dream Merynne went to the window. Frank was walking down the garden path. He disappeared through the gate, but returned minutes later.

He would, of course, she told herself bitterly, to ensure she didn't harm his bastard – his love-child.

As if she would. She couldn't hurt any young thing. All she wanted just then was never to have to look on him again.

*

A sufficiently well-educated girl called Emma Hayne was found to take charge of the children. She came of a worthy middle-class family in Penjust whose father had died, leaving her mother and herself practically penniless. Having gone through a brief training as a governess, but unable to complete the course owing to financial circumstances, she had advertised for a post suitable for her limited qualifications, and luckily for all concerned, Frank had heard of her, and after a brief interview had engaged her on the spot, without consulting Merynne. She was small, slightly built, but with a determined set to her chin and clear grey eyes that could be intimidating in their straight stare. Her manner was gentle, her voice soft and clear. There was a grace and fawn-like quality about her movements which belied an inward strength of character that Merynne sensed immediately she saw her. She'd been annoyed at Frank's temerity in going ahead with arrangements, and not asking her own opinion concerning the girl, but knew there would be no point in argument. From the first day of the baby's – Laurette's son's – arrival at Tarnefell, Merynne had continued to ignore the child's existence as much as possible; this had meant that even Luke was left more in the charge of the daily girl, and saw far less of his mother than previously.

As for Bethany – Bethany was puzzled. The entrance of the new baby into the household, and her mother's disregard for it, made her watchful and at times withdrawn and quiet when before she had been boisterous and full of pranks. She knew something was wrong somewhere. Her father even was not quite the same as he had been in the past. He didn't laugh so much, or pet and spoil her as he once had. She no longer felt she was his 'princess' or that she particularly mattered to him. Of course, he was always nice to her when he was round the farm or in the house, but he was very often away, and there were long hours when he shut himself in his room seeing no one. At such times Bethany's chief comfort was her young dog Leo, a present from Wellan on her last birthday.

The truth was that Frank's financial problems were mounting. Emma's wage, on top of other expenses, was more than he could properly afford, and he was having to face the unsavoury fact that there was no way of making a quick fortune from farming. The adventure of it was beginning to seem an illusion. His other enterprises had always held excitement, and the stimulus of knowing that each day could bring wild success. Tarnefell promised only hard work – maybe years of it – before he regained a part of what he'd spent. His agent was cautiously optimistic.

'A matter of time,' he said. 'You can't force the land.'

And Frank glumly thought back to his days in Africa, where hacking and digging and forcing could bring such undreamed of riches at a moment's notice.

If his relationship with Merynne had been more satisfactory his inherent optimism and vitality he might have viewed the picture quite differently. But although she gave physically and uncomplainingly what he desired of her body, it was as an automaton, holding herself inwardly remote and chill.

Once, following intercourse, when he tried to embrace her, she dragged herself from him with such unmistakable contempt he flinched, and with an angry gesture sprang from the bed.

'I'll leave you to your sterile company,' he said bitterly. 'The affection of my dog will be far more rewarding.' He paused at the door, glanced round at her where she still lay, back turned to him, her hair flowing over the pillow. 'Well, madam?' In a rush of anger he turned, put both hands on her shoulders and forced her to look at him. Her face was very pale, her eyes cold clear pools of resentment. She could have been some ice-maiden from a fairy tale.

His grip tightened momentarily, then suddenly loosened. 'I suppose you know I could divorce you,' he said, 'for your unspeakable attitude?'

'Oh no, Frank. The boot's on the other foot, and you know it. Or Roland wouldn't be here, would he?'

'You can't forget,' he said, more heavily, 'that's the trouble. Just because of a child – a small defenceless creature needing care. What sort of a woman are you, Merynne?'

'Not very brave, I'm afraid,' she answered, still in the emotionless manner he'd become accustomed to, 'or I should have left, with Luke, long ago. But I'd nowhere to go, had I? And then there was Bethany. But why go on about it? I never deny you anything. You can't complain – sexually. And I've no doubt by now that even if I did, you'd easily find someone else to oblige. Maybe you have already. It doesn't matter to me in the slightest.'

The cutting remark stung him to action.

He pushed her over and slapped her smartly twice. 'You – you hypocrite,' he said, through rising despair and anger. 'There are worse things than adultery – murder of the heart – and by God you're an adept at that.' He broke off, put a hand to his forehead, then turned and looked at her again.

Her lips were curiously tight and hard. Two bright spots of colour now burned on her high cheek bones.

'I've never hit you before,' he said heavily, 'but you asked for it, and if you expect an apology, forget it. In future remember just where you stand. I'm master here, and intend to remain so. Think about it.'

He went out, banging the door loudly and walked quickly down the landing towards his own private sanctum, leaving her lying rigid in the large bed.

She didn't sleep that night. Her senses were too disorientated, and shamed, filled with humiliation and a secret triumph at the same time.

She'd hurt him, and was glad of it. But the knowledge was strangely ungratifying. If only he'd approached her differently – allowed the baby Roland to be placed in some decent foster home, she'd have been able, in time, to see his affair with Laurette in more reasonable perspective. His presence in the home had been a constant reminder of the unsavoury incident – a wedge in their marriage causing only bitterness and resentment. Deep down Merynne recognised her jealousy and meanness – knew also that no one in the world, ever, would matter to her as much as Frank, the Nat of her youth and lover of her young maturity. All she wanted was reassurance, the conviction that he still loved and desired her as he had in the past. But he gave her no chance. There was no way of assessing his true feelings, and during the past few months she'd come to the conclusion all that mattered was over between them. Nothing remained but her own pride – a stiff determination to retain at least what was morally more hers than his – Tarnefell, and her son Luke's – Will's child – the right to inherit. This other infant, the bastard intruder – could have no legal claims whatsoever, neither would Bethany, being a girl and born after Nat's desertion by taking off to sea.

Her life and what affection remained in her therefore, must be concentrated on Luke. The trouble was she was no longer very personally involved with him. Emma had proved herself sufficiently capable of taking responsibility for the children on her own shoulders.

So Merynne was left to plan her days as best she could, attending to minor household duties – duties that didn't much interest her – brooding over her own inadequacies and Frank's infidelities, while he moodily surveyed the future with worrying distaste.

And a year after they'd moved to Tarnefell, disaster occurred.

19

Roland, in Emma's charge, thrived, to the delight of Bethany. In the baby she sensed something of her own rebellious spirit, and at seven year's old that spring of 1824, made it her business to be part guardian of her young half-brother. Luke didn't interest her. He was still frail, and by that time even Merynne began to accept the doctor's opinion that he was 'backward', both physically and mentally, though she didn't say so. To look at he had a delicate, fey beauty – almost girlish – that was misleading until he was addressed or asked questions. Then he more often than not merely stared without answering, as a dazed empty look clouded the blue eyes. Sometimes he went into passions for no logical reason. His feelings for animals was unpredictable, except for the dog Leo. He might destroy a butterfly if the mood took him to do so, although he saved crumbs to feed mice in the cellar. At four years old he could speak in only short sentences and Emma who was giving Bethany lessons grew day by day more doubtful that he'd ever be normal.

She was cautious, but honest with Merynne and Frank in her own assessment of his potential. Merynne thrust her chin out stubbornly.

'I don't accept her opinion,' she told her husband one day scathingly. 'What does Emma Hayne know about four year olds? And he's barely that. Calling him a simpleton –!' She broke off indignantly.

'She didn't,' Frank retorted quickly. 'She just pointed out, like the doctor, he was slow. Compared with Bethany –'

'How can he be compared with Bethany? She's older, and too forward by half. But of course she's your idol, isn't she?'

He touched her shoulder. 'Merynne, *please* –'

She shook herself free, turning her head away so he wouldn't see the glimmer of tears in her eyes.

'Leave me alone,' she said shortly. 'I don't want to discuss the children. It was *your* idea to have Emma. If you hadn't given her complete authority I should have had more influence with the children. As it is – Luke's missing a mother's care, that's all.'

'And who's fault is that?'

She didn't answer, merely looked away and walked from the room.

Following the unhappy conversation, Merynne made an effort to become closer again to her young son, and loving as she had once been. But he did not respond. The consequence was that the little boy became a source of irritation and contention between Frank and herself.

'I think Bethany would be better at school now,' she said one day bluntly. 'She'd have discipline, and not be able to upset Luke as she does. You say Luke's backward, but he knows how you feel about Bethany. Then Roland –'

'Yes?'

'Since you mean to keep him here, he'd be better without a restless young girl forever fussing over him. She and Emma between them are completely spoiling him. You don't see it, because you won't. But when he's older there'll be trouble. I'm warning you, Frank –'

'And I'm warning *you*. Bethany's going to no stuffy boarding school. She wouldn't like it, and I can't afford it. There! that's the way it is. I'm doing my damnedest to make a living from this place. It's not easy. But I intend every child here to have an equal chance –'

'Including Luke?'

'If he's capable.'

'I *see*! He has to prove himself.' Her tones were bitter.

'A miracle if he can.'

'Oh. So you think that.'

'I'm afraid I do. You'll have to accept it, now – or later –
that the boy's lacking.'

'*Lacking*?'

Suddenly losing patience, Frank said, almost shouting,
'Yes. It gets more obvious every day. Let's hope when he's
older he'll be fit to cut a hedge or use a hoe. You'd better
pray for it, Merynne. Otherwise –'

'Go on –'

He shrugged. 'I was going to say, "Better he'd never been
born", but that wouldn't be right I guess. Most living
creatures have a use somewhere. I hope to God we find one
for Luke.'

Merynne was outraged.

'That's a terrible way to talk. Beastly. It just shows what
you are.'

His underlip tightened ominously. 'Exactly. And as
you've no more illusion left I'll prove it in another way.
You've asked for it a long time.'

She glared at him mutinously.

'Upstairs with you,' he continued, speaking more brutally
than he'd meant. 'Do you hear me? Or shall I carry you –'

'Don't be ridiculous. With Emma about? And the boy? –
then there's –'

'To hell with them.'

He stepped towards her. Suddenly realising he meant what
he'd said, she hurried past him, paused briefly at the door
before going through, then with a semblance of dignity in
case anyone was lurking about, lifted her skirts daintily
above her ankles, and walked with head up, along the hall to
the staircase and her bedroom. He followed.

She walked to the window and turned to face him.

'Well?'

Slipping the key of the door into his pocket, he said,

over-casually, 'It's high time I had a glimpse of your luscious body again. So will you kindly oblige and remove those stuffy petticoats.'

At first she didn't stir. Her heart had started to thump painfully. This was no longer the Frank Wellan she'd grown accustomed to lately, but the Nat of long ago, confident, domineering, the young passionate lover of her youth, but far more formidable.

'Frank, I –' she got no further. One arm was suddenly round her, the other wrenching the bodice and skirt of her gown open. Every nerve in her body was quivering with a range of mixed emotions – anger, indignation, fear, hatred, and a dark deep desire for him, stronger than all the rest.

When she stood at last naked, except for a pair of lace-trimmed pantaloons, he first pulled the combs from her hair, leaving it tumbled about her pale shoulders, then firmly loosened the frilly drawers. She bent down to retrieve them as they fell, but he swept her up with his arms and carried her, though she was kicking, to the silk covered quilt where she lay rigid and still.

He stared down on her, with a lop-sided smile on his lips, at the same time unfastening his neck-scarf, shirt, and trousers. Then his body was close over hers; she felt a hand touch her temple caressingly, moving slowly over the high bone structure of her cheek, and down the satin-smooth column of her slim neck to the curve of breast and downwards to her thigh. His lips traced every part of her, savouring her sweetness. Then suddenly the excitement in him accelerated to a wild pitch of passion that took her without restraint or consideration.

'Well?' he said afterwards, with forced brightness, 'I hope you enjoyed it.'

She did not reply, and he had no way of knowing the dull disappointment that filled her – saw only what he mistook for contempt on the lovely face. 'She despises me,' he thought bitterly. 'She's still hankering for that pie-faced oaf of a farmer.'

When she didn't speak he continued, 'You'd better get up and make yourself respectable. I apologise for ruining your well-ordered day.'

'But, Frank –'

'No need to be polite or make excuses,' he retorted, putting his shirt on savagely. 'You've mastered the art of putting me in my place very well indeed.'

'I said *nothing*,' she protested. 'I can't understand you. If you just want an argument –'

'*I don't*.' He sat down again and pulled at his breeches. 'I'm darned sick of moods and eternal talking. And in future let us leave the children out of marital argument. Bethany's no longer an infant, and she's bright. We don't want her unhappy again. It's our business to keep up a charade of affection in front of her.' Actually there was no need for pretence. Bethany, who'd happened to be in the hall when the argument started had paused, hiding herself behind a curtain, and overheard most of the heated conversation.

Part of it registered painfully. The words – her father's – 'the boy's lacking', followed by 'better he'd never been born'.

They'd been talking about Luke. Luke was the cause of the rift between her parents. And yet it wasn't his fault, she told herself honestly, with an odd feeling of pity. He'd been born kind of funny, and papa had said something else to. Something about 'a miracle'. Perhaps if there could be a miracle like there were in books, Luke could be well and happy, instead of always making her mother sad and cross and her father miserable. In fairy tales such things happened. She knew now that fairy tales weren't always true. But once, when she was only Luke's age, they had seemed to be. She'd found such magic then. Maybe that's what Luke needed – a bit of magic – the kind of magic Torgale had. *Torgale*! he was just an old stone really, everyone told her so.

But perhaps he could come alive again for a little boy like tiny Luke.

Once the suggestion was firmly planted in Bethany's mind, it flourished to reality. She'd take her young brother to see Torgale. No one need know. There were times when Emma couldn't *always* be with him. Roland had to be cared for and fed now, and sometimes when he screamed for his food Emma had to rush from the nursery to wherever his cradle was, and pick him up and soothe him. Luke was left alone then. There wasn't much danger of him wandering away, usually. His legs still weren't very strong, and he preferred to be with his toys, or in the kitchen where the dog lay by the stove. If she was specially nice to him, and gave him one of the lovely lollipops that papa brought her from Braggas, he'd do what she asked and creep out, just as if it was a game, when the grown-ups weren't looking.

So for the next few days Bethany planned, and waited; waited for the opportunity for Torgale to work his magic on Luke.

The chance came three days later when the weather changed unpredictably from warm spring to lashing gale-force winds that by afternoon had become intensified. The morning had started comparatively calmly, with only a slight breeze ruffling the sea and moors. The sky, not yet properly clear, was lit by streaks of blue, but the coastline and distant rim of hills were too brilliant, too intensely dark and glittering for peace ahead. Looking over the Atlantic was rather like staring at a painting too vivid to be real. Bethany, who had been secretly brooding over the unsatisfactory relationship between her parents felt stimulated suddenly by a desire for action. Surely there was *something* she could do. She wasn't a baby any more – and life at Tarnefell could be so exciting and happy if only other people were happy too.

Luke – poor little Luke – was the cause of the quarrelling, of course. But it wasn't his fault that he was small and shy

and had sudden queer moods. Perhaps if he could be
'magicked' – as she had been when she was his age –
everything would be changed, and he would be a *real*
brother to her as Roly would be when he'd had time to
grow. Already a bond was deepening between herself and
the exuberant Roland, Laurette's child. But years had to
pass before he was old enough to go wandering and
climbing the rocks with her. During that time anything
could happen. Mama and Papa might part. That was a
dreadful idea. She wouldn't be able to bear it, she just
wouldn't. So something had to be done about Luke.

Watching the quick interchange of light and shade across
the landscape – of sudden wild clarity disappear into
darkness then lift up again as the sun splashed its brief
radiance over the scene, she thought of Torgale. When she
was a tiny girl Torgale had given her such happiness,
dispelled in a few moments any frustrating mood or feeling
of being unwanted and criticized by her mother. Just an ugly
old stone that had been there for ages? – yes, very gradually
she'd come to accept the truth. But Luke was still very
young. Perhaps old Torgale *did* still work magic for tiny
things. Perhaps if she took Luke to him, and wished hard –
why, she could even write a note! – perhaps the spell would
work again. Grown-ups would laugh at her for thinking
such a thing. But grown-ups didn't know everything.
Sometimes they were very stupid, blind to the secret world
she knew so well.

Once the idea of asking help from Torgale occurred to
her, Bethany wasted no time in putting the plan into action.
First she wrote a few words to the menhir, then went to look
for the little boy. He was dropping pebbles one by one into
a bowl on the nursery floor. When the container was full he
threw them all out with a rattle, laughed wildly at first,
before starting to cry. Bethany took his hand and whispered
in his ear. The sobs ceased. He looked up, wide-eyed and
beautiful, not fully comprehending, but realising his

half-sister had something 'nice' to show him.

The wind was rising when they crept down the stairs, and out of the side door. No one seemed about at all, just as though they wanted to help, Bethany thought, although she knew they didn't. Emma was busy with Roly in the bathroom, and Papa was out. Mama had been in one of her anxious moods all day, which meant she'd been busy with a number of small unimportant things, and not really interested in the children at all. The new cook that Frank had engaged recently, because she herself had 'more than enough to do already' – Merynne's own words – was occupied with baking and making pies in the kitchen. So it wasn't really difficult for Bethany and Luke to slip conspiratorially from the house to the path leading up the moorland slope. The hills were brown and dark now. As they climbed the wind increased quickly, sending a spatter of dead leaves whirling from the sombre branches of bent trees and bushes. Luke stopped and would have run back, but Bethany put her arm round him and urged him on.

'It's magic,' she said, opening her cape and drawing him close. 'Torgale's magic. Come on, Luke. Look at him – he's waiting.'

The little boy stared upwards towards the ancient stone; everything else except the menhir, seemed to be moving. Clouds blew and raced in darkening shapes against the stormy sky, but Torgale stood lonely and defiant, impervious to the elements swirling round the carved granite face. Bethany pulled Luke close, still holding his hand tightly, then she laid the note down under a stone.

'Do you know what I've put?' she shouted against the gale which by then was moaning through heather and gorse. 'I've said "Please deer Torgale make sum magic for Luke. Make him strong like me. Make Mama nise to Papa –" '

The little boy shivered and pulled. 'Home, home,' he said, trying to turn, but Bethany wouldn't release him. She stood with her dark curls tossed free in the air, gazing upwards at the cold primitive countenance. Below them – far below – the sea tossed in heightening fury against the gaunt cliffs where a French brig *Louise* laden with cotton, brandy, wine and tobacco floundered against the jutting Pike Rocks bordering Cragga Cove. Casks of rum and other goods were already floating and being tossed towards the shore while the crews struggled to regain control and save the ship, but the vessel was quickly going to pieces when Frank, with the help of coastguards and farm workers, made an effort at saving what human life was possible.

Bethany, concentrating only on Torgale and Luke, was quite unaware of the wild scene, and everyone at Tarnefell was too concerned with preparing blankets, hot soup, and aid for survivors, to realise, at first, the absence of the two children.

Luke grew peevish. 'Cold –' he moaned, 'cold – cold.'

Tears were running down his face, mingling with rain then driving across the moors. Bethany, disappointed by Torgale's lack of response, grudgingly turned to go back to Tarnefell, but the elements had such force and fury, she almost lost her footing, and moved instead close to the stone. She leaned against it, drawing her brother close. With her head bent over his she undid the cape at her neck so more was available to cover the fragile body.

'It's all right,' she whispered, 'it'll soon be over. Torgale won't let it last long.'

Her teeth were chattering. She knelt down, but got up after a short rest and forced herself to make another attempt. A gust of freak wind so strong that even the earth seemed to shudder, blew her back again, and she fell, striking her head hard against the granite. Consciousness remained sufficiently long for her to ease her body half over Luke's, giving him all the warmth she could from her closeness. Then darkness encompassed her, taking her to deep forgetfulness, in which life became a fading dream of images slipping at last to rest.

Luke's thin wail, mingling with the high cry of a lone gull filled the air. Presently, as quickly as it had risen, the storm died.

The little boy was still screaming fitfully when they found him half an hour later. But the violent blow on Bethany's temple combined with exposure, had put her forever beyond human help.

Frank, who'd been alerted by a shepherd, knew it at once, when he reached the scene.

With pain and a wild bitterness in his heart, he carried his young daughter – his princess – to the house, where three survivors from the shipwreck were already huddled in the kitchen. A farm hand followed, with Luke in his arms.

There was silence when they entered a back room. Merynne gave a long look at her daughter, then turned to Frank.

'She's dead,' she said. 'She's dead, isn't she?'

Frank nodded, slowly and dumbly.

Even then Merynne's eyes were dry, her shock and grief too strong for outward emotion.

Frank laid Bethany on a bench, drew a blanket over her and took his wife gently by the arm.

'Come along,' he said automatically. 'You can do nothing here.'

She pulled herself free and went to the door. 'Leave me alone,' she said. 'Just leave me.'

Frank sighed and returned to the little boy who was being forced to drink hot broth by Emma.

Of all the ironies of life this was the worst he'd ever encountered. He guessed that Merynne would hold Bethany's death against him, and had to face the fact that Roland, now, might be all he possessed of his own in the world.

*

For some time, as might have been expected, no scolding

word left Merynne's lips, no wild accusation, or blame for anyone but herself.

'It was my fault,' she said simply one day to her husband. 'I shouldn't have married you.'

'What on earth are you talking about?'

'It was a judgement. Because of Will.'

He could have shaken her; but her eyes were so sad and solemn, so filled with despair he hadn't the heart.

'Don't talk that way. Forget Will, for Pete's sake. You've got something of him left anyway.'

'Luke?' There was a taunting note in her voice.

'That's right. He needs you more than Bethany ever did; *and* you know it.'

Yes, she did. But any passion she'd once had for the handicapped boy seemed to have died in her. With him it was the opposite. After Bethany's tragic death his eyes took on a haunted look, following her, whenever she was near or went out of a room.

'He misses his sister,' Emma remarked one day, with a hint of reproach in her voice. 'I think he's lonely.'

Merynne glanced briefly at Luke. 'Perhaps. But I'm sure he'll get over it. He has his pets. He's always liked animals better than people. Fetch him his box of treasures. That'll occupy him.' With which casual comment she went.

Emma sighed, left the lusty Roland gurgling on a rug on the floor, and fetched Luke's box out of the cupboard. She knelt down and took the lid off. It contained an assortment of things – pebbles, a tin toy soldier, an artificial flower from one of Merynne's discarded gowns, feathers, shells, and even a piece of seaweed from the beach. There were other articles too, including a crumpled smudged piece of paper.

'What's this?' Emma asked, trying to straighten it out. 'A letter?'

Luke nodded. He didn't explain, or even try to – that Bethany had written it out before copying it more neatly as her request asking Torgale to work his wonderful magic.

Emma scanned the childish words with pity rising in her.

'... please deer Torgale make sum magic for Luke ... make Mama nise to Papa ...'

She broke off reading. The rest of the note had been scrawled out, re-written, then scribbled over again. But the signature was clear.

'Bethany.'

'Can I keep this for a while, Luke?' she asked. 'You can have it back later.'

The little boy nodded absently. The letter no longer meant anything to him.

A little later Emma located Frank at the stables. Since Bethany's death he'd found that riding only could provide any real relief for his feelings. He looked tired and haggard when the girl held out the piece of paper.

'Well?' he queried sharply. 'What's this?'

'I thought you should see it,' Emma said quietly. 'Mrs Wellan's in her room – resting, I think, and I didn't want to disturb her.'

'Hm!'

He took the memento, scanned it closely for several seconds, then asked sharply. 'Where did you get it?'

The girl told him, adding, 'She thought a lot of that old stone. But you must have known. It was a kind of fairy tale – escape for her –'

'From what?'

Looking away, Emma answered, 'From other people's arguments and misunderstandings. Bethany wasn't made for quarrels. She was meant for happiness. Everything she felt and saw had some kind of – of tremendous wonder and importance. She called it magic. But I suppose a man wouldn't understand such things.'

'Do you indeed! That's just your opinion,' he said. Then more politely. 'Thank you for showing me. I shall give it to my wife of course.'

'Naturally.'

The door closed.

A moment later Frank's footsteps could be heard disappearing down the drive towards the house.

20

Bethany was buried on a still, golden day, in a far corner of Braggas churchyard overlooking a copse of larch sloping down to a stream. It was a simple ceremony, attended only by members of the house and farm, and a few miners who still held respect for Frank Wellan and what he'd try to do for them. They felt, as well, a sense of loss over 'the little maid's' passing. She'd been popular with the locals – effervescent and cheerful as the moors and Cornish skies – skipping and laughing one moment, the next solemn as any young owl.

All agreed it would have been far better if the boy – Will's boy – had been taken. Sad, they said, that he should be the one left, lacking as he was, in the head.

Neither Merynne or Frank showed their feelings outwardly, though Wellan did his best following the funeral to comfort his wife, without demanding anything of her. To make love, he knew would have been solace for many women, but though she allowed him to touch her hand in a gesture of friendliness, and was with him in his grief, Merynne's inner core remained withheld. It was as though she was encased in tight armour allowing no contact with the outside world.

This new assured Merynne with the pale tight lips and cool manner was far more intimidating and difficult to understand than the unpredictable young woman she'd previously been. Emma respected but didn't trust the veneer.

'It's not natural,' she said to Cook. 'It would be better for her to go riding with Mr Wellan, to take a holiday somewhere. Self control like hers is bound to break sometime.'

'Well, she shows no sign of it yet,' came the reply. 'In fact I've never seen the mistress more industrious. Busying about the dairy – seeing to the laundry – even giving orders to the stable boy when she feels like it. Then all those goodies she's told me to make – they're not for the farm, you know. She's a fancy to go visiting – to some of the families that've no work, because of Wheal Chace. Part of it's been closed already, and they say more men'll be unemployed soon.'

'I didn't know that.'

'Why should you? You don't mix with locals. Not that you've time; you've more'n enough to do lookin' after they two boys without chattin' about the countryside.'

Yes, that was true, Emma agreed to herself; but she was still worried about Merynne.

As events proved later, she had every reason to be.

On an afternoon when pale sunlight filtered only thinly through a quivering haze of mist, Merynne set off on a young mare, Folly, with a saddle bag of food strapped behind her, containing meat pies, a chicken and other sweetmeats and savouries. She rode astride as she'd learned to do following Will's death; her destination was a cottage only a quarter of a mile from Wheal Chace, and two others further on, huddled in a fold of the moors. The autumn weather had turned chill. Families lacking breadwinners now, would be in need of nourishment to help them face the prospect of winter ahead.

Knowing this, and feeling that she was being of service helped, momentarily to ease her sense of frozen guilt. Bethany would have approved. If Bethany were alive she'd have wanted to go with her – Bethany! Frank's princess! – Bethany, *Bethany*! the damp wind seemed to moan and cry her name through the grey air, flapping monotonously against her face and ears – Bethany, Bethany. With an effort Merynne forced the illusion away, kicking her mount to a sharper speed. Boulders, lumps of heather, and wind-blown bushes passed in a vista of changing twisted shapes, dark against the uneven browned surface of moors and bog-holes; as they continued, the looming silhouette of mineworks ahead showed intermittently, wreathed by vaporous cloud and smoke. Realising she had to cut up to the right to find the cottage, Merynne headed her horse in a different direction, and as she passed a clump of clawing black elder, something shot up like the darting head of an immense snake, to intercept her.

At the same moment an ancient rough voice screamed, 'Away with 'ee gorgio. Curses on 'ee for the deaths of my grandchilder – those of my own blood. Curses on 'ee I say –' The grating tones died into a jargon of Romany, as Folly reared, front hooves pawing the air.

Merynne, struggling to control the mare, was almost thrown, but managed to retain her seat. Giving free rein to Folly they plunged ahead, taking a haphazard route to the coast. As they cut down a narrow ravine a glitter of silver ahead showed that the tide was in. The pale sands below the black cliffs quivered fitfully, shadowed by looming shapes of rocks piercing the breaking tide. Merynne reined, stayed for a few moments in the saddle, then dismounted. Sensing freedom, the young mare broke away, and with a snort of delight was galloping along the line of sea and shore until a bend in the cliff obscured all sign of the flying form.

Merynne wiped the mist from her eyes, stared disconsolately round and called the horse's name. There was no response. The bag of goodies had fallen, leaving the contents strewn about the sand. There was nothing she could do now, but climb back somehow up the ravine and find her way back to Tarnefell. The mist was thickening. She was uncertain how far she'd come. Her only guide would be the mine, when she located it. It must be somewhere above, but distance was deceptive in fog, and the locality was a lonely one filled with patches of bog and treacherous shaft holes. She shivered, not only through quickening fear, and a sense of apprehension, but chill.

She had only scrambled a few yards up the gully when a slide of stone and rubble was dislodged from above. There was a sudden roaring sound, a spasm of acute pain as a sharp piece of granite crashed against her head. Then she fell. A bird screamed shrilly, followed by a man's shout. A burly figure emerged from a cave set deep under the rock. He was bearded, wearing a fisherman's cap and jersey and carried a pail of bait in one hand. No features were visible through the grey light, but from his gait, and attitude, he certainly wasn't old. He stood pondering for a few moments, staring at the recumbent figure of the girl. Then he bent down, and lifted her up in his great arms.

She gave a little moan, that was all. The light had already darkened during the last few moments. At the end of the short tunnel there was a bend in the track. He laid Merynne down and kindled a glow from a candle in a glass bottle. Then he managed to get a spitting fire going.

His dwelling was roughly converted from natural formation into a crude dwelling place. There were shelves, a table, chair and a bed made up from wreckage that he'd brought in from the beach. Fishing gear was heaped in one corner, and everywhere was permeated by a strong smell of salt and oil. Nothing was visible to the outside world. 'Big Joe' was seldom seen except for rare occasions at a seaman's kiddleywink where he bartered a catch for rum. Little was known of him except that he had appeared apparently out of nowhere two years back, and made a living as best he could by fishing in his small hand-made boat, or occasionally catching a rabbit on the moors. No one asked questions, or answered any, if enquiries were made concerning a wanted naval deserter. Big Joe was useful on occasions, and the Law wasn't popular in these parts. The recluse could be a help in certain smuggling or wrecking operations. If he'd committed a murder in the past – and this was the story – then no doubt the victim had asked for it, and good luck to Big Joe.

Eventually all search had been given up. No one anymore would recognise the swarthy, rotund and begrizzled recluse as seaman Joe Blaize. He was taken for what he had become, and 'odd fellow a bit strange in the head', but nevertheless not one to cross. A good ally when needed, who could be a bad enemy when betrayed.

So nobody spoke of him at all.

Alone he lived; alone he was content.

Until he found Merynne.

*

She woke from a strange deep dream, feeling curiously peaceful, although when her senses returned her mind was a blank. She could remember nothing. Looking round, her surroundings gradually registered. The walls were of granite, covered in places by old pieces of tapestries and sailcloth. She was lying near a glowing fire, covered by a blanket. Odd shadows streaked round the interior; from somewhere quite fifty or a hundred yards away a thin streak of daylight filtered, died, then expanded again with a zig-zagging line. The boom of breaking waves echoed in a constant hollow thud. Further down the passage or cave, the lemon gleam of lamplight crept to meet the dawn. She eased herself up; her hair was loose, and fell in a pale cloud about her shoulders, covering the wound which had been carefully washed and dressed. The pain now was only slight. She lifted a hand to it automatically, and at that moment the man approached her from the fitful shadows. He was carrying something in a crude earthenware bowl.

Porridge.

He leaned down, pushing it at her.

'Take it,' he said. 'It'll do you good.' He didn't smile. His deep set eyes appeared expressionless beneath the shaggy brows, the mouth was unsmiling above the stubble of beard.

She accepted gratefully.

He didn't frighten her; there seemed nothing unpleasant about him, and she was still too dazed to bother about how she'd got there or who she was.

'Thank you,' she said.

A flicker of pleasure changed his expression briefly but in an instant had gone.

'Reckon you've come at last,' he said. 'My woman. Is that it?'

When she didn't answer he continued. 'You don't know?'

She shook her head.

'Hm!' he stroked his chin. 'Well, we'll see. It's all right anyway. You bide here s'long as you like. A nasty fall you had.' He paused before he added, 'Can you cook? Fry a dab? Skin a rabbit?'

'I don't know.'

'You don't know nothing, do you? – Well maybe you'll learn.'

She frowned in bewilderment, looking down at her near-naked body beneath the blanket.

He turned away, coughing gruffly. 'I'll find you something to wear. Those things you had on weren't no good for round here.'

'What clothes did I have?'

He gave a short laugh.

'Innocent as a new born babe, aren't you? But don't you come questioning now. I don't like questions. Treat me right, and you'll be safe with me. Big Joe'll take care of you.'

His gaze softened and darkened as his eyes probed into hers – clear and luminous as the small sea pools outside. He touched her hand gently.

'Don't you worry,' he said.

And strangely, at that moment, she didn't.

21

As the pain of her wound eased, Merynne's mild headaches died into an acquiescent acceptance of a state half-dream, half reality, in which fragments of memory rose then died again, before they could make sense. For some days she was content to lie in her unknown refuge, safe from prying eyes or contact with anyone but Blaize. She was warm, well fed, and mostly content. He did not attempt to question or intimidate her, and was mostly silent in her presence. On occasions she caught him looking at her with an odd questioning look in his eyes. He had lived so long free of women that conversation between them seemed impossible.

To him, at first, she meant little more than a wounded animal taken into care. He fed and cooked for her, noting with dumb satisfaction faint colour return to her cheeks, and life to her eyes. He saw then that she was beautiful, and once touched the silken sheen of her hair with a rough hand. She didn't flinch or frown, and that pleased him. In a way she'd become to him a treasure, like a mermaid, washed up by the tide.

He'd called her 'his woman', but the term had signified nothing sensual. Reality and the urge of life in him was concerned with day-to-day existence – taking his boat out to fish, labouring about his secret domain, collecting firewood, and sometimes doing odd manual jobs at the kiddleywink a mile away. During his first days in his retreat he'd had a goat, but the animal had attracted attention, so he'd sold it to a smallholder in the district. To keep completely to himself – to be a 'loner', was, he'd discovered, the best and safest way for a man in his position to live.

Finding Merynne had been a shock. His first instinct was to carry her to the inn and let the landlord do what he liked with her. Second thoughts had restrained him. Zachary Pellan was a sly, greedy character who'd soon have his way in any fashion he chose with such a defenceless young creature as the one who'd fallen in Joe's own path. And she wasn't all *that* young either, he'd realised after a close look at her. Her lips had a tired droop about them, and there were faint lines round her eyes that suggested she'd suffered. Zachary mightn't've wanted her for himself anyway. He might easily have delivered her to some ruthless slaver for good gold in his pocket. Women of class and looks were always wanted for brothels and harems abroad.

Then what to do with her?

The answer was only clear in his mind when he found she was witless. Not wrong in the head exactly – she was too lovely for that, but half dumb and without memory. He'd keep her for himself so long as it was safe. She could learn to cook, and 'do' for him when she was recovered. Then, later, maybe nature'd do the trick, and she'd come willing to his bed. He hadn't anticipated ever having a woman close again. But he wasn't old – there was still strength in his loins, somewhere desire lingered, though he was happier maybe without such complicated factors. Whichever way things worked out he'd not force events. She could bide till she wanted to leave, or until someone came to look for her.

Curiously, Merynne had no wish to leave. Joe Blaize afforded her comfort, shelter and peace, for which, after a week had passed, she gave her services in return, frying his fish when he returned from hours at sea on his boat, mending his clothes with primitive needle and thread provided, and seeing his washing was done regularly.

'Like a wife you are,' he told her one evening, as they lounged in the hidden part of the cave by the glowing fire.

'A long time since I thought o' having a wife.'

The word 'wife' disturbed her, though she couldn't have said why.

Noting her frown he leaned forward and touched the satin smooth line of cheek. 'What's the matter, woman? Don't you like me then?'

She nodded reluctantly. 'Yes, I like you, Joe. It isn't that.'

'Then what? Why do you shy away?'

'I don't know. I don't mean to.'

Disappointed, he shrugged, got up, and remarked. 'That seaweed ought to come in. I'll go and fetch it now. You go to bed if you want. I'll not disturb you.'

Knowing she'd hurt him she got up and touched his shoulder tentatively. 'Don't be angry, Joe. It's just – I must have come from somewhere – even now –'

'Come from somewhere? *Course* you did, like all things do – rabbits, goats, pigs, even fish from their mother's belly. But where's your mother now, girl? And what use?'

She turned away.

'I wish I could remember.'

'Why bother?' he said gruffly. 'Living's for today.'

He was right, of course, she told herself when he'd left. There was no use in trying to probe or think; her mind wouldn't work. Something had happened to bring her here. But what, she'd no idea, except that there must have been an accident. When she questioned the man, it was always the same, he'd told her more than once, 'You're all right, aren't you? Your head's better. You have good food and sleep. What more does a living creature want?'

She had no answer to that. At nights, it was true, she was too tired to bother about anything. But as time passed she began to envy him when he strode out each morning to his boat.

Freedom!

The longing to be free and sail away when she felt inclined, as he did, either to fish, or for pleasure, became an urge in her. That particular piece of hidden coast assumed for her the feeling of being in prison. Except for her memory she was physically fit, yet he forbade her to leave.

Why?

'Take me with you,' she said, on the twelfth day.

His eys glinted dangerously. There was a mutinous thrust to his chin.

'No.'

'Why not?'

'Too dangerous. Men about.'

'Men? What men?'

'Those who'd harm you. You stay quiet here and do as I say.'

The curtain of her mind stirred slightly, shifted, letting the image of a face clarify briefly, then fade before she could bring it to proper perspective.

Joe's sullen expression died.

'Arent' you happy here?' he said, 'I haven't harmed you in any way – not wronged or beat you. I like you, girl; know that, don't you?'

She sighed.

'Oh yes, Joe, and I like you, of course I do, but –'

'Not enough though. Is that it?'

The deepening of colour in her cheeks, her softened pleading look, were answer enough for him.

'I'm sorry, Joe. Really I am.'

He turned away stiffly.

'You needn't be. My own company's been enough for me for many years now. Reckon always having a woman about isn't quite my line. Don't you worry – we'll find out about you soon as possible. I'm not aiming to have any bit of skirt round my heels who's not the heart for it. In any case you ain't the type.'

Rebuffed, she bit her lip, feeling for the first time since her accident a rush of undignified emotion.

Joe had bought fish back for the evening meal, and

Merynne was preparing it, when she was disturbed by the excited barking of a dog. The man who was mending a net at the far sea-end of the cave shrilled, 'Hey you! What d'you want here? Off with you.'

But the shaggy yellow shape streaked past him, rushing down the tunnel to the cave's hidden living quarters.

Merynne gasped. Without thinking, she cried, 'Leo – oh Leo! –' The joyful animal bounded up and almost knocked her down as his wet tongue covered her face between shrill squeaks of recognition.

Blaize strode heavily down the passage.

'Who's this then? Know the animal, do you?'

'*Know* him? Of course I do. It's my dog – *our* dog, I mean –' she floundered before adding, 'Bethany's. He was Bethany's really –' The walls of the cavern seemed to sway, the floor to move slightly, while memory flared, ebbed, then settled with slow painful awareness. She was about to fall but the man's arm was about her waist, steadying her.

'Sit down,' he said, gruffly, easing her to a settle. 'Don't talk now. Later you can tell it all. I'll get this dog a bone –'

He turned his back on her, leaving her alone with the animal. Gradually the dog's excitement eased. He pushed his nose over her knee giving occasional yelps of pleasure, liquid brown eyes gazing up to hers, while his shaggy tail still wagged intermittently.

The return of memory was both relief and agony to her.

When Blaize returned, knowledge – the experience of her past life with Nat, Will, of child-bearing and loss through death of her daughter – had swept, temporarily, all girlhood from her face. Innocence had fled. He sensed in those fleeting seconds the stark truth of the despair that had drawn her to him. She could never have belonged – never really been his. The lovely creature he'd rescued and cared for had only been a shell of the real self. It was a mercy he'd discovered it in time. A woman would have complicated his whole existence away. Why – he no longer even wanted her, not as she was, haggard and lost in memories. The fragile beauty he'd briefly savoured had been no more than a glimpse of sun through cloud, as meaningless as a froth of foam flung glittering into the air.

Funny he should think of things that way; poetic somehow, like the dreams of a youth without his feet on the ground. Well, *his* feet were placed firm enough; and the sooner he got his own place to himself again the better. There'd been a time, before he joined the navy and met with trouble – when he'd fancied himself as a bit of a scribe. He'd soon learned better. Dreams were for fools; and he was no fool. The sea – sun, rain, hard work and the simple life were all he wanted, and he was damn lucky to have them still after all these years.

He looked at the woman speculatively.

'Reckon you've properly come to yourself now?' he said.

She nodded.

'I'll have to go back, Joe. Back – home.'

He nodded.

'Course you will. I never aimed to keep you here. You just tell me where you come from – your real name an' I'll get word somehow.'

Half an hour later, dressed in her own clothes that Blaize had kept stored away, Merynne, guarded by Leo and Zachary Pellan, waited at the kiddleywink while Joe took the nearest route to Tarnefell. He knew, and the landlord knew, there'd be a reward for the safe return of Mistress Wellan.

Joe, to Frank's surprise, would have none of it.

'I want no payment for living things,' he said bluntly, when they got back to the inn. 'You just let me be and forget about all this.'

Frank shrugged. 'But –'

'You heard what I said, mister.' Joe turned and strode away into the fading evening, a dark figure disappearing against the rim of moors and sky.

Frank still hesitated. 'A queer customer,' he said, after a pause.

'That's right. But you'd best do as he says,' Zachary commented. 'He's one on his own, Big Joe is.'

With which comment Frank had to agree.

*

Frank had never felt so mentally exhausted in his life before. Sickness, fevers in the past, accidents, fights, and brawls in the gold-fields had left his body racked and feeble for a time, but he had been young then, and underlying exhaustion, his fighting spirit had never failed, had always surfaced eventually with new optimism and vigour. Now, facing Merynne once more, he savoured the first pangs of defeat. He hardly recognised the fragile tired-looking woman as the girl he'd so often taken in passion, loved, lain and laughed with, fought sometimes as any strong male does with the wilful spitting female of his choice.

She didn't even attempt to argue with him, or shift a portion of their mutual tragedy on to his own shoulders.

All she said, when Blaize had left, was, 'I'm sorry, Frank. I didn't want to be such a trouble.'

His normal reaction would have been to take her in his arms, and somehow bring warmth to her body, an outburst of emotion that would have stimulated something of the old relationship between them. But when he touched her arm, her response was to draw away, and add lifelessly, 'I'm very tired. I shouldn't be. Joe was very considerate. He did his best for me all the time, and I felt all right. It was when I remembered –' she put a hand to her forehead. 'If Leo hadn't found me –'

'Well, he did,' Frank intercepted firmly, 'and you've got to try to put things behind you now. It won't be easy. It's not easy for me either. But I reckon Bethany would have hated us to be miserable. And we've the other two to think of.'

'*You* may have,' she said pointedly. 'Oh – forget I said that –'

'No. We're going to face things squarely. Young Luke

may not be bright, but you bore him, and he's a handsome little lad. With training, and interest he'll be able to enjoy life. Then Roland! – you've got to accept him, Merynne. In time maybe he'll be closer to you than Bethany ever was.'

Her lips quivered.

'You shouldn't have said that.'

'I should've said it earlier.' His voice was grim. 'She never knew where she was with you. I've got to take half the blame for that. But there's no point in going over the past. Bethany's gone. Every second that ticks away thousands die somewhere – it's the pattern of things – coming and going, dying, living – we're all part of it, and for us it's life. *Life*, Merynne. So for heaven's sake try and look on the cheerful side – enjoy it while you can. You need a good rest right now; tomorrow everything will appear different.'

'I hope so,' she said.

He sighed, and glanced towards a desk where a pile of papers stood. Her eyes followed him. 'What's all that?'

'Work. I shall be dealing with it half the night I guess. Getting Tarnefell into order's swallowed up more capital than I thought. But from now on it should be possible to see a little profit. The herd will have to be kept to a minimum though. I've burned my boats a bit there. Still, if anything happened to me you'd be all right.'

'What do you mean? If anything happened to you?'

A hint of the old mischievous smile lit his face briefly. 'What I say, love. *If*. But don't worry, there's a good deal of life in this old dog yet. It's you I'm concerned about. Now get yourself off to bed before the doctor comes, or I shall have Emma on my heels. Oh. And just one more thing –'

'Yes?'

'Take a look in at the boys as you go. I've a hunch young Luke's been lonely.'

'Oh, I don't think so,' she said. 'Not for me.'

'I didn't say for you. What's it matter who for? Loneliness can be hard for a kid at any time. And it's my belief he frets for Bethany.'

Without a further word she left him, went upstairs, and called in at the bedroom where the baby and Luke now slept.

Emma was just about to leave.

'Everything's ready in your room, Mrs Wellan,' she said. 'There's a fire going, and your sheets are heated. I hope you sleep well. Luke –' she glanced towards the small bed where the little boy was already sitting up, watching, '– here's your mama.'

Merynne moved towards him, forcing a smile. How beautiful he was she thought, – remembering paintings on Christmas cards of cherubs. But what was the use of looks without mind or feeling?

To her surprise he said in soft high tones, 'Mama.'

She went towards him, but he drew away instantly, cringing and pushing a hand under his pillow.

'What is it? What have you put there? One of your toys?'

He drew his small fist out, and held it towards her grudgingly.

'Moony. It's Moony.'

As she peered down curiously his fingers uncurled, revealing the small pointed nose of a mouse. Whiskers quivered beneath the tiny bright eyes.

Merynne gasped.

'*A mouse?* In bed? But it mustn't be. Here –'

Luke clutched the tiny animal to his chest.

'Go away,' he said. 'Mine. This is *mine*. Moony.'

Just then Emma returned.

'Did you know about this – this creature?' Merynne demanded more sharply than she'd meant.

Emma nodded. 'Oh yes. He's a great friend of Luke's. In a minute I'll be taking him to his cage in the storage cupboard. It may seem an odd arrangement, but saying "goodnight" to Moony has become an evening ritual. It's only for a few seconds, Mrs Wellan. He's a very –' she smiled whimsically, '– well-trained mouse.'

'I didn't know there could be such a thing.'

'Luke has a way with pets,' Emma said ambiguously.

A minute later the mouse had been removed.

Merynne automatically kissed Luke's cheek, then, surprising even herself, she turned and took a look at the baby's cot.

A rush of mixed emotion churned in her. He was so like Frank, and yet he wasn't hers. How was she going to get used to the situation? This was the boy she should have borne – robust and healthy, with Nat's look of challenge already in his bright dark eyes. He suddenly took a thumb out of his mouth and smiled at her. She looked away abruptly and walked to the door. Her head was a whirl of confusion. The reaction of shock caused a fit of trembling she couldn't control. Emma, back from returning Moony to his cage, met her outside the door.

'You're tired,' she said, 'and no wonder. You should have left the children till tomorrow.' She paused before continuing, 'Don't worry about the mouse. He isn't usually allowed in Luke's bed. This was a special occasion. A birthday treat just for a minute or two!'

'A *birthday*? Whose?'

'Moony's. That's what Luke told me. "Moony's birthday", he said. "I want him". So –' she shrugged – 'I didn't see any *real* harm, just for once.'

Merynne forced a faint smile. 'You must know best.'

She allowed Emma to accompany her to her bedroom without further remonstrance. All she wanted by then was to flop down and rest.

She was already sleeping when the doctor arrived half an hour later. After a brief examination he assured Frank his wife had apparently suffered no ill effects from her experience. He prescribed a potion, rest and freedom from worry. 'Tomorrow, or the day after, she should be back to normal,' he said. 'I'll look in next week some time.'

As easy as that, Frank thought wrily, watching the man pick up his bag, smile politely, and nod in his characteristic encouraging manner. But of course it wouldn't be easy at all. The deeply seated pain and resentment still lingered in Merynne's heart, and might do so for the rest of her life.

As for him –!

Frustration, defeat, emptiness following the loss of Bethany, roused a sudden savage desire for activity in him. He needed purpose, something more than a farm to work for. There was young Roly, of course – a bastard, with no legal claim – he had responsibility there. The boy mustn't suffer because of Merynne's attitude.

Merynne.

He loved her still. She could have been his mainstay – the heart of his existence and endeavour. They were both comparatively young. Together they could venture into new spheres, conquer new worlds. But he doubted she'd understand. Well, why should she? Tarnefell was her home. To her it meant the past as well as the future. To him it signified, now, mostly bitterness because of the loss of their daughter. A man couldn't live fully with bitterness for company.

Then what?

Although he didn't properly realise it himself, Frank Wellan was already becoming Nat Herne again – forever the adventurer, on the brink of some wild unknown dream.

*

By the spring of 1825 the farm was showing a modest profit. The Wellans had become accepted as respectable, if modest, property owners in the district – even acknowledged by minor members of the Cornish gentry, who were aware of Frank's potential for 'getting on'. It had already been suggested in certain circles that he might have reasonable support in standing for Parliament. There was talk once more of another old mine being cleared of water, and restarted. Wellan was not the type of man, of course, to be admitted openly to the *best* circles, but anyone capable of supplying employment to a considerable portion of the working community, was worthy of respect. Food and work meant contentment in the district, with no riots or trouble from the new unions which could be such a thorn in the flesh of the gentry.

At first, the suggestion of becoming a political figure had titillated Frank's fancy. He had presence, fire, and a certain capacity for oratory that might cause many a skirmish in the House. Coming of working stock himself gave him a right and the power to speak up for the ordinary man.

But did he want that? Having to listen and deal with boring jargon that fundamentally had no interest for him? And the finance! – to live as colourfully as he fancied during his inevitable periods in London would take more than he had now to get by on.

There would be times when Merynne would want to accompany him, and that would mean added expense. If he could be sufficiently extravagant to give her the life of a great lady! – the princess he'd once envisaged, dressed in silks and satins, the envy of other women with her jewels and furs – then it would be a different matter. But he didn't fancy the mediocre existence of having to scrape and plan just to get by. Once he could have savoured town life in the grand manner. But circumstances and his own foolhardiness over the Ring Theatre had wiped the possibility out. What he secretly wanted – although he as yet didn't admit it to himself – was to get away once more – somewhere right away at the other side of the world where he could use his sweat and guts to make a fortune all over again, returning at last to provide a future worthy of his lovely Merynne, and all the best for the two boys, especially his own, his son.

Would Merynne want it though? Did she *really* want him any more?

Sometimes he doubted it. Day by day she appeared to be

becoming more serene, more practical, so acquiescent and obliging in her moods – even in bed, he was puzzled and a little in awe of her graciousness.

He knew he shouldn't feel that way. He'd given her all she had that was worth anything – a manor-type farm instead of the small working one run by Will Drake – help in the house, anything she asked for, in reason, and since his one lapse with Laurette, complete faithfulness.

Maybe he was a fool over the latter. Sometimes women lost interest when they were too sure. But – oh hell! he thought whenever his mind ran along these lines, it shouldn't be necessary to use such reasoning. Once, with Merynne there hadn't been. They had been fire and ecstasy, warmth and life to each other. Laurette, was it? Was she the cause of the rift? No, it had started earlier than that. He was darned if he could pin-point the exact cause, except resentment on her part for his ever having left, and he'd thought that to have died long ago.

Although she didn't speak of it, Merynne was aware of his growing unrest, and mistakenly took it for a lack of interest in herself. Her looks were beginning to fade, she told herself whenever she glanced in a mirror. Her face, having lost the first bloom of youth, was thinner, and since Bethany's death she'd lost weight. Her aptitude for enjoying the pleasures of nature – of walking, riding, savouring the sweet wildness of the moors – the scent of brine and heather and brush of fresh wind on her face – was losing impetus. Once, when she'd felt the urge of freedom, she had been able to put household matters behind her, forget farm duties and the routine of everyday life, and for a brief spell become a girl again, capable of unrestrained emotions, of laughter and tears, giving, taking, quarrelling on occasions but always eventually losing bitterness in the joys of forgiveness and making-up.

Now she and Frank no longer even had their scraps or impacts of temper.

Where had all the life gone?

It couldn't only be Bethany. She and Frank had been close
– so sweetly, wildly close, long before Bethany's begetting.
Children weren't necessarily the mainstay and root of a
marriage – merely the fruit of it. Time after time she told
herself this, and was sad because she could find no solace in
Luke or his half brother. Any dislike she'd felt at first for
Roly, died gradually during that summer, but she could feel
nothing for him. She was a woman without emotional
purpose, and the knowledge flattened her.

One evening when she was least expecting it, Frank strode
into the bedroom. He was wearing night attire.

'Look here, Merynne,' he said, going to the bed and
bending over her, 'it's time we came to an understanding,
don't you think?'

She glanced up at him, her eyes wide in astonishment.

'What do you mean? Frank, what's the matter?'

She didn't really need to ask. Obviously he had been
drinking more than he ought. His face was flushed, and he
was breathing quickly.

'Nothing very obtuse,' he answered. 'Just a glimpse now
and again of my wife's body, and proof she's still available.
Lusting in vain for ever isn't an occupation I enjoy. Perhaps
for once –' a hand slid to her shoulder, then downwards
over a soft breast, where it lingered, tightening its pressure
till she flinched.

'You're – you're –' she couldn't finish. His mouth was hot
against her cheek.

'Drunk? Is that what you were going to say? Well –
hardly. Just slightly inebriated, perhaps. Because that's the
only way I have nowadays of mastering sufficient courage to
approach you, my darling.' The 'darling' had a sarcastic
ring to it.

Confused, wanting yet rejecting him at the same time, she
struggled against him.

'Please don't be like this. Another time –'

'Another time, another time,' he echoed. 'Damn it! Haven't I waited long enough? Watched your cold little mind criticise and condemn, seen the steely glint of your eyes when you so coolly conceded your favours. Look at me, Merynne. *Look* at me.'

He forced her head up, staring into her face, noting only the strained look on it, sensing more of the bitter-sweet longing in her heart.

'Yes,' he said hiccupping. 'You can't disguise it any more. You dislike me, don't you – hate the touch of me. Well, madam –' his voice hardened. 'If that's the way it is I'll have you in hate and to hell with your pleas and cries and don'ts and oh Franks –' He broke off for a second while her mind whirled in a tumult of defiance and turbulent despair. Sense or truth no longer registered. In the warring bond of hatred and love they were united, and when it was over there was only a brief pause before he swung himself from the bed, and reached for a wrap.

At the door he swayed a little, turned and said, 'I'm *most* obliged, thank you, my dear. Our little session was most revealing.'

More than anything else in the world at that moment she wanted to fling pride away and rush after him, somehow bring him back and in a torrent of words bridge the gulf between them. But all movement seemed to have deserted her.

'He'll come back,' she told herself. 'He *must*. We can't go on like this. Whatever he is – whatever I am – I *want* him.'

But he did not come back, and in the morning she found a note from him saying he'd left for Plymouth, and would be away for a week.

22

The day was windless and sultry, overhung with a yellow sky through which the sun was only a blurred amber behind a grey haze. Not a blade of grass quivered. In the fields the few cattle huddled by the stone walls as though sheltering from storms to come. A cloying sweetness filled the air, redolent with the scent of roses, tired flowers and heather, gorse, and the distant tang of woodsmoke from the moors. Foxgloves drooped and sheep rested by boulders where an occasional adder was coiled above the browning bracken.

Merynne felt an intense loneliness, as though Frank had gone from her forever. She wished it would rain. The constant chirping of crickets from the garden and droning of bees and flies about the borders unnerved her. When she picked a few late blooms for the house, gnats hovered round her in a cloud. She returned to the lounge listening, and then there was a stir of commotion from the kitchen. Footsteps hurried down the hall. Glancing round Merynne saw Cook rubbing her hands on her apron, with fear on her usually placid face.

'I'm sorry, ma'am,' she gasped. 'I've got to go. It can't be helped. I'll have to leave the cooking to you, it's all –'

'Whatever's the matter?' Merynne demanded. 'Do please calm yourself and explain.'

'There's a fire at the mine, ma'am – Wheal Chace. The engine house or sumthen, I doan' know. But men are hurt, and Bob, my son – he works there. I've got to go and see what's goin' on. He may be dead for all I know –' She broke off, breathing quickly.

'Are you *sure*?' Merynne queried. 'Certain it's not just a rumour? There are moorland fires at this time of year and –'

'Oh I know, I know it's true. Billy Bream's at the door with his vegetable cart. He'll take me there. Heard of it through Tommy Paynter's Joe. Joe works at grass. *He's* all right, but I got to go.'

Merynne could do nothing but agree.

When the woman had gone she went to the kitchen where the daily girl was staring round bewildered at the dishes to be washed and the baking only half prepared for the oven.

'You'd better get on with what you can for a bit,' she said. 'I'll tell Mice Hayne to try and give you a hand. I'll be back presently.'

'You haven't by any chance –' she paused before asking bluntly, '– you haven't seen the master anywhere have you?'

The girl shook her head.

'Oh no. Except that – he went off early, said he was getting the coach or train or sumthen for Plymouth.'

'Thank you.' So Frank had done what he'd said, and would know nothing of the mining disaster – if what Cook had stated was true. Not that he'd be involved financially. All Frank's commercial interests in Wheal Chace had been severed a time ago. Still, it seemed wrong somehow, he shouldn't be there. Wrong, but a relief to her that he'd be safe himself. Following this thought the harsh truth of their misunderstanding and apartness registered again with chilling bitterness. Once they had shared everything. Now it seemed the bond had died.

A quarter of an hour later, after a brief consultaion with Emma, Merynne wandered back into the garden, wondering if any sign or glow of distant fire could be seen. Only a lurid deepening of the sky in the mine's direction was visble. But it was enough to verify Cook's statement. In the past she herself would have been anxious to be on the scene, giving what help she could, but all motivation for human feeling at that point, seemed to have deserted her, leaving only emptiness and inertia.

Without consciously realising where she was going, she left the garden and took the path towards the moors and Torgale's wild domain.

The air was still sultry. Generally, nearing the first ridge there was some freshening of air, a fanning of sweetness against the face, or faint rustle of undergrowth. But that day there was nothing. No sound but a sudden flutter of bird's wings, and crackle of undergrowth where she walked. As she neared the stone, a faint glimmer of sun pierced the haze. Almost instantly it had gone again. Merynne wiped a strand of hair from her clammy forehead and then – she saw it. A crouched small figure by the foot of the menhir. He was seated on a flattish boulder and was glancing up with motionless concentration at the ancient relic's gnarled face. There was a small box-like article by his side. A hand, palm upwards, was raised as though in offering.

Luke!

At first Merynne thought she must be suffering an illusion – the effects of her recent strange experience. She rubbed her eyes but the child was still there. She took two cautious steps forward; he didn't stir, but horror froze her nerves for a tense moment. On the lifted hand was a crumpled piece of paper, and on it was curled a slender reptilian shape with flat head raised elegantly on its long lithe neck. A snake! whether slow-worm or adder she couldn't tell in the shifting light, but she sensed the latter.

In that moment of realisation, caution was temporarily forgotten.

'*Luke!*' she said in a half whisper. 'Luke!'

Slowly he turned his head. There was a faint smile on his lips. Dew glistened on his bright hair and lashes. He could have been a fairy creature from *The Tempest* or some ancient fairytale.

Then he spoke.

'Mama.'

There was a gentle movement.

'Sh!' she cried, 'don't move; be careful. Stay there, Luke –'

But the little boy, without fear, gave a flip of his fingers and the snake slid off gracefully on to the short turf, disappearing a second later behind a rock.

Merynne gave a sigh of relief and rushed forward drawing the slender young form to her. 'Oh Luke – Luke! You *mustn't* play with snakes. Hasn't Papa told you? I was so frightened –'

His eyes widened in astonishment.

'Mama? Frightened? Moony isn't. Moony – Moony –'

Wonderingly, she glanced at the little cage on the ground. From inside, the small mouse was regarding her with bright eyes, trying to poke his nose at the crumpled piece of paper outside the wire bars.

'What have you got there?'

Luke handed her the note. But it was more than a note. Tiny drawings of figures such as a young child might do, were standing hand-in-hand in a line. There were three of them – matchstick-looking depictions with long legs, and at the end one smudgy dot. Attempts at writing had been added, but the letters, except for a large M and P, were undecipherable.

Merynne screwed up her eyes then turned them again upon her son. 'Did you write this Luke? Are the drawings yours?'

He nodded.

'Mama – Papa, me too.' He pointed to the smallest figure. 'Me. There's Roly,' indicating the dot.

'But – but *why*? What –?'

The beautiful guileless eyes regarded her unblinkingly.

'Magic,' he said. 'Torgale's magic. All of them magicked. Together. Altogether. Papa, Mama, me, Roly. Not Bethany. Bethany's gone.'

His lip quivered suddenly. He stood up holding the mouse lightly under one arm. 'Moony's tired.'

He turned, sobbing softly and started, half stumbling, to take the track back to Tarnefell.

Then Merynne understood.

Poor, sad little Luke. He'd been fretting for his sister, and not only for Bethany, but for the rest of them, as she had, because there was no joy in the house, and he had sensed in spite of – perhaps *because* of his handicap – the bitter relationship between herself and Frank. He'd wanted them to be friends, warm, loving, *together*.

Oh God! What had she and her husband between them done to this one small lonely scrap of humanity, except to drive him for comfort to an old stone, Bethany's sanctuary? Torgale, whose only magic was a reminder of days long long ago when an ancient people had believed in symbols of their own primitive imaginings?

She followed the little boy quickly and put an arm gently round his waist.

'Come along,' she said. 'Maybe Torgale's magic will work. If it doesn't, I know something that will.'

'What?'

'You wait,' she said, 'wait like Bethany did, for *her* magic. Things don't always happen at once. You just have to wish and *wish*.'

Gradually they drew nearer to Tarnefell. Once she glanced back. The air seemed to have freshened, a sudden ray of dying sunlight lit Torgale's granite face, then died again behind misted cloud.

What had she glimpsed in those few seconds? Nothing really, except changing light and shade on old stone. But ever-deepening knowledge filled her – a realisation of the hidden potentials lying sleeping somewhere in the hearts and minds of most human beings – especially the innocent and lost.

When they entered the house, Emma was in a turmoil of

anxiety, holding young Roland in her arms.

'Oh thank heaven Luke's with you,' she exclaimed. 'I only left him for a minute because Roly started screaming, and with the fire and Cook going so suddenly –'

'Don't worry,' Merynne said. 'Everything's all right. And everything's *going* to be,' she added firmly, 'from now on.'

The words were bravely said, although she knew even when she spoke them, that where Frank was concerned things might not be as easy as she hoped.

*

Wellan did not return until late that night, and by that time, although his mind was at rest concerning business affairs and the confirmation that Tarnefell was properly on its feet, free of any debt or foreseeable future problems, he was both bored and weary. At Braggas he'd intended to fortify himself with a drink before facing Merynne, but at the last moment had refrained. What was the point? Liquor was only an antidote for frustration, which, in an hour or two, would find him at low ebb again.

So he'd continued the journey, and when he reached Tarnefell the house was in darkness except for lamplight in the hall and a flickering glow from above – his wife's room. The knowledge that she still might be awake didn't please or interest him. The titillation of her presence that had once held such allure now only mildly irritated him because of the arguments following. He was sick of trying to probe her mind and the complications of her quicksilver memories – her reproaches, reserves and wayward moods. Bethany's death had become a further unseen wedge to any understanding between them. What the days ahead would bring to them both he couldn't fathom any more; neither did he want to. He just wanted to get on with his life simply, without emotional conflict. The passionate interim of the night before had been a mistake. Thinking of the inevitable reactions on her part, made him inwardly wince. Therefore when he walked along the landing and saw a chink of light flicker under her door he quickened his footsteps and would have passed unseen to his dressing room if it hadn't opened slightly revealing a shadowed glimpse of her figure.

'Frank –' she said quickly.

Instinctively, he paused. 'Yes? Is there anything you want?'

The abrupt question chilled her, but she answered with flurrying urgency.

'Yes – oh yes. I want to talk. Today something happened. I –'

'Oh God! you mean the fire? I heard on the way back. Now isn't the time to talk, Merynne. You should be asleep, and I need an hour or two. Go back to bed for heaven's sake –' He was about to go ahead, but she grasped his arm, saying breathlessly, with her heart pounding:

'This is *important*. It concerns you – *you*.'

He sighed. 'What the hell – oh very well. But no dramatics if you don't mind. During the past months I've had more than enough.'

He followed her into the bedroom. Candles were flickering on the dressing table, an oil lamp by the bed cast an interlaced rosy glow of streaking light and shade over the carpet, furniture, and the subtle curved flimsily clad figure confronting him.

He stared: what on earth was she up to? As he approached closer he couldn't help noticing that every lovely feature she possessed – delicate sensuous lines of throat, lips, and tumbled brightness of her hair – the shadowed beauty of her eyes, and enticing curves of her sensuous body had somehow been enhanced as though for an artist's painting.

He rubbed his eyes thinking at first he must be mistaken.

But when he glanced at her again he saw he wasn't. She was smiling, faintly provocatively, yet warmly, as she had not done for years. The diaphanous thing she was wearing was that of a mistress, a nymph, rather than of a wife.

Following his first astonishment a quick surge of anger combined with irrational unwanted desire, seized him.

'What are you trying to do?' he demanded. 'Seduce me?'

Lifting her chin up she moved toward him and reached both hands to his shoulders.

'Perhaps,' she admitted. He removed one hand firmly.

'Then don't, Merynne. After so long it's not –'

'Suitable?' She shook her head slowly. Her voice, though emotional, was sad, when she said, 'Oh, Frank, don't push me away. It's not been easy for me – all this. If I hadn't – hadn't – loved you so much –'

'*Love?*'

'Oh yes, yes.' She pressed her face against his chest. 'You know it. We both know it, don't we? Haven't we always –? Or – don't you care any more?'

Suddenly his defences dissolved and crumbled into capitulation, and his two arms were round her holding her so tightly that breasts, ribs, waist, buttocks, the whole of her, became crushed into a pain that was both agony and a deep wild joy.

'Frank –' she let out a sigh, feeling a spot of blood on her under lip. 'Do love me –'

There was a pause. Struggling for self-control, he managed to say with a ring of hardness in his voice, 'Then take that thing off.' He jerked the flimsy nightdress from the neck down, letting it fall to her feet in a frothy heap. 'And wipe your face of that – that stuff,' he said, pulling a handkerchief from his pocket and doing it himself. 'I don't aim to take a woman – especially my wife – looking like some whore from a brothel.'

They were both trembling when she stood at last, lovely as any legendary young goddess in her nakedness, unpainted and unashamed.

Then very reverently he lifted her up, and let his lips travel from hers to throat, breasts, thigh, and the triangle of gold, her womanhood, where they rested briefly, before he carried her to bed.

When their love-making was over, they lay in complete peace for a time, until, with one hand still cupping a breast, he said, 'Now perhaps you'll explain, and tell me what's happened; the truth – the whole of it, my love.'

And as the new dawn slowly lit the sky, she began.

23

When Merynne had described her experience with Luke at the menhir they both lay for a long time in silence. It was as though some conflict of misunderstanding between them had flared at last to its climax, then died into a strange acceptance of the inevitable. Wellan took her hand and said, 'I see. You've discovered after all that the boy has feelings. Well, that's something for you – for both of us – to begin on.'

'What do you mean? Begin?'

Slightly embarrassed, he said, 'To think less of ourselves and more of the youngster I suppose; – we've done a hell of a lot of demanding and talking and prancing and playing about with our lives and emotions, Merynne. Maybe the time's come to stop all that and get down to brass tacks, find out what we really are –' His voice faded on an enigmatic note.

She frowned slightly, puzzled.

'What do you mean by that?'

He gave a short laugh.

'Darned if I really now – not the whole of it. It's what I've got to find out, about myself, and you too. Nothing'll ever change what I think of you; I love you. But there's millions of other human beings existing on this little earth of ours, and I've a feeling sometimes we should know more about them –'

A touch of fear gripped her.

'You mean you want to go away?' Her voice was tight, low-keyed.

'That wasn't in my mind exactly, at this moment. I wouldn't take off leaving you and the two boys on your own, but we've got to widen our spheres somehow, love – see more through the eyes of other folks, so we don't make the same mistakes again.'

'About the children, you mean?'

'Oh they come into it. Luke anyway.'

'And Roly?'

He glanced at her face in the half light.

'Roly will be all right, I'll see to that. But it's important you accept him as one of yours – *ours*. You're the only mother he's got – same as Luke.'

'It isn't quite the same as Luke,' Merynne said quietly. 'He had Laurette. If it wasn't for her –'

'Yes, I know. I know. If I hadn't taken what she offered that night he wouldn't be here at all. Oh, don't let's go over all that again, Merynne. You've always resented what happened. It's natural in a way, but –'

'*You* haven't, have you?' Merynne demanded bluntly. 'If you had the time all over again the same thing would happen, wouldn't it?'

'Yes, if you acted in the same way you did then,' he told her shortly. 'As for regretting –'

'Well?'

His hand stole up her arm and tightened near her shoulder, 'Oh damn it, darling, how can anyone in their senses regret a lusty, bawling young thing full of health and laughter and a hunger for all the things life's for –?'

A tight little ball of pain knotted her throat.

'The trouble is, Frank, you'll never be able to feel that way about Luke.'

'No. But I'll feel *differently*. He'll be *considered* more. Somehow I'll give him the one thing he needs – to feel *wanted*, Merynne. He's not all that – that lacking, you know. You found that out yesterday. Underneath his oddness there's imagination. And imagination's one of the best gifts any kid can have, given a proper outlet.' After a short pause he continued in firmer, more practical tones, 'Let's drop the subject now, shall we? We've a family under our noses to care for, then let's do it. And maybe a bit for those others too.'

'You mean the fire? The miners' wives and their families?'

'Yes.' He left her suddenly, pulled on his clothes, and went to the door.

'I should've been off earlier than this,' he said. 'And if it hadn't been for you, you lovely creature, I'd have spent the night there.'

'How can you *say* that, after what happened?'

After three quick light strides he was back by the bed, kissing her.

'Because I'm a man, love, and you're a woman.' He grinned. 'Sometimes priorities get mixed up. A woman's business is her home. But a man's –' His face darkened. 'Out there – there's work to do. Not my responsibility, practically speaking, but things I know, situations I can deal with – concerning ordinary bereaved and injured folk. And I know you won't try and stop me. Mrs Wellan you may be, but underneath I'm still Nat Herne – into any tom-fool difficult and dangerous bit of work that comes his way.'

Yes, it was true, she thought, Nat; he was still Nat, and she wouldn't, deep down, have had him act in any other way.

She smiled.

'Go on,' she said, 'off with you. I've things to do, too. My hair's a sight, and I must see how Luke – how the children are.'

The look in his eyes, a blazing glance of gratitude and love, told her all she needed at that moment. Whatever happened in their lives from then on, nothing would ever lessen the enduring bond between them.

*

Two years passed. Tarnefell, under the agent's and Frank's

surveillance, had by then become an established manor farm which, though comparatively small in relationship to the larger Cornish estates, was acknowledged and respected by influential land owners.

Merynne was content in her life. Roly, through his overwhelming vitality and charm, had won her affection, and Luke was proving that Wellan's optimism and faith in his inherent ability was not misplaced. He was poor at lessons, his learning capacity in that direction was useless scholastically. But he developed an inborn capacity for understanding nature and animals, and was never happier than when one of the men explained some simple task that he could undertake with his own hands.

'He'll never be clever, of course,' Merynne remarked a little wistfully to her husband one day. 'It's no use trying to make me think so. He's –'

'He's got his own kind of cleverness,' Frank told her, 'and that's what's needed here. When they're older Roly and him'll make a fine pair. Physically too, he's a credit.'

The latter was true. Luke Drake was a handsome boy, straight as a young buck, fair as a legendary Viking, with eyes that in idle moments held an enigmatic quality as though searching distant shores. Mostly he seemed happy. Occasionally he wandered away on his own for an hour or two, but he'd learned the dangers and landmarks of the terrain, and Merynne was wise enough not to show anxiety.

There was only one shadow on her horizon – something she'd had to learn to live with during those rich years of 'coming together' – the niggling fear that one day Frank would want to take off again. She knew the old restlessness still seized him sometimes – could feel it even after love-making, when he assured her he had everything in the world he wanted – '*Everything*,' he said once, 'except more for you, my love. More fine things – more jewels and comfort – everything on earth that's worth finding I want for you –'

'But, Frank, I've *got* it,' she protested. 'Don't you understand? – you, the children, Tarnefell –'

'Yes, I'm glad for you about that – Tarnefell,' he said ruminatively.

But she sensed he still had something on his mind, the old demon he'd been born with – that had been Nat Herne's.

And in the autumn she knew.

One afternoon she was standing in the garden with a spray of burnished leaves and chrysanthemums in her hand for the house, when she chanced to look upwards to the rim of moors stretching brown and gold against the clear sky. A distant figure, dark on a dark horse, was poised motionless facing the sea. He had one hand to his forehead, and could have been, momentarily, a figure carved from granite. Her heart gave a little jerk. The pose, somehow, was so indicative of longing – of a desire for freedom such as a prisoner might have, after being confined for years.

Nat.

It was Nat she saw there – no longer Frank Wellan – but the man he'd always been beneath the ambition, the achievement and apparent content – the explorer and adventurer – for ever searching for new worlds to conquer. The 'gipsy' and the King in one.

Her love.

In that moment of revelation she knew she could keep him at Tarnefell if she set her mind on doing it. He loved her and would never leave against her will. But in one sense his purpose was finished there, at least for a time. The farm was on its feet. Financially she and the boys were secure. In tying him to her she could lose the most previous thing she'd ever possessed – and she wouldn't be able to bear it.

As she watched, a small blue butterfly settled on her hand for a moment, then flew away, brushing her cheeks with its wings as it passed. And she remembered the poet's words – Blake was it? – 'he who kisses the joy as it flies, Lives in Eternity's sunrise'.

Still looking upwards she saw the horse and rider turn, and canter along the ridge until their shapes had disappeared behind a hillock.

Slowly she went back into the house. The afternoon sunlight was already fading into blurred and dying gold.

A blackbird sang.

How strange it was, she thought, that sadness and joy could be so curiously intermixed.

*

That evening when they'd gone to bed Merynne managed by subtle means to draw the truth from her husband.

'Well, yes,' he admitted at last, when she'd put the final question. 'I *have* been a bit restless lately. Not for myself only – as I said, for *you*, my love. There's a project abroad I'm interested in – mining, where I could be of use and make a packet – a real fortune, sweetheart. It'd only be for a time – a year and a half perhaps, and when I came back –'

She lifted her fingers and pressed them quickly against his lips. 'Oh, Nat – *don't* – please don't go on. I *know*. I've known for weeks – months perhaps, that you were fretting, and I understand, I do really.'

His eyes widened in astonishment. 'You *do* – and you don't mind?'

Although the tears were near falling, she managed to hide them.

'Of course I mind; I love you, Frank, and because of it I don't want to chain you. I know one day you'll return, and then –'

His arms tightened round her.

'And then, by God, you'll know what it is to have a *real* man for a lover,' he told her. 'Not just a farmer of property, content to sit on his backside until old age.'

She managed to smile.

'That's something you'd never be,' she told him.

He grinned. 'No. I guess you're right.'

So it was that a month later Nat Herne once more set off for the Americas.

She saw him off from Falmouth, and waved as the *Fair Maiden* moved from the harbour towards the open sea.

Then she slowly made her way to the carriage that was waiting for her, in the town.

Emma was there, with the two children, who had accompanied her for the outing.

'Papa gone?' Luke enquired.

'Yes, darling, for a little while,' Merynne replied, trying to sound matter-of-fact, 'so you'll have to look after us now.'

'I will,' the little boy replied, with a radiant smile, 'and Roly too. And I'll find another Moony.' There was a pause until he continued, 'It'll be nice to have another Moony, won't it?'

Merynne nodded.

'Very nice,' she said.

Under the rug, Emma's hand found hers and held it comfortingly until the vehicle left the town on its return journey to Tarnefell.